There was blood.

Cassandra's worry started to climb again, but Jones was all eyes on her.

"Are you okay?"

All she'd done was swim a little, use her emergency tool a little more and then tread water. She was fine physically.

But, man, her emotions were rough.

The blood on his head, his completely soaked clothes, the image of him not moving in the driver's seat?

What if Cassandra hadn't been there?

Would he have made it out?

Or would he have died, at the bottom of the creek, never knowing...

It was all too much and Cassandra did the only thing that she could think of in the moment.

"He's yours," she blurted out. Her hands went to her stomach. "The baby. He's yours."

RETRACING THE INVESTIGATION

TYLER ANNE SNELL

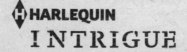

This book is for Ashley Parr. You're the best dang social worker
in the world, and without your guidance and compassion helping
us through a wild ride, this book would have still been a thought
in my head. Thank you for making us a family.

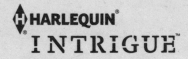

ISBN-13: 978-1-335-58202-7

Retracing the Investigation

Copyright © 2022 by Tyler Anne Snell

Recycling programs
for this product may
not exist in your area.

Harlequin Enterprises ULC
22 Adelaide St. West, 41st Floor
Toronto, Ontario M5H 4E3, Canada
www.Harlequin.com

Printed in U.S.A.

Tyler Anne Snell lives in South Alabama with her same-named husband, their artist kiddo, four mini "lions" and a burning desire to meet Kurt Russell. Her superpowers include binge-watching TV and herding cats. When she isn't writing thrilling mysteries and romance, she's reading everything she can get her hands on. How she gets through each day starts and ends with a big cup of coffee. Visit her at www.tylerannesnell.com.

Books by Tyler Anne Snell

Harlequin Intrigue

The Saving Kelby Creek Series

Uncovering Small Town Secrets
Searching for Evidence
Surviving the Truth
Accidental Amnesia
Cold Case Captive
Retracing the Investigation

Winding Road Redemption

Reining in Trouble
Credible Alibi
Identical Threat
Last Stand Sheriff

Manhunt
Toxin Alert

Visit the Author Profile page at Harlequin.com.

CAST OF CHARACTERS

Sheriff Jones Murphy—Retuning to Kelby Creek and picking up the mantle of sheriff, this single father and widower begins to reinvestigate the town's most infamous case. But it isn't until he has an unexpected reunion with the woman he hasn't stopped thinking about, pregnant with his child, that he realizes the danger and stakes have never been higher.

Cassandra West—This kindergarten teacher is wary of fate until she's saved by a handsome sheriff who happens to be the father of her unborn child. Reunited and immediately in danger, this Kelby Creek transplant joins the hunt for the truth and the fight to survive.

Annie McHale—The investigation into her kidnapping and then disappearance seven years prior changed the entire fabric of Kelby Creek. Now all eyes are turning back to the case that started it all.

Carlos Park—The right-hand man to the sheriff will do anything to keep the destruction after Annie's kidnapping from happening again.

Jimmy Wheeler—This co-owner of a local restaurant isn't happy about the sheriff's investigation and no one knows why.

Unknown Man—Someone is lurking in the shadows and has a much bigger plan for the town, starting with the sheriff and his loved ones.

Prologue

Annie McHale's disappearance was the beginning of the end for Kelby Creek. They hadn't known it then. Not when the town helped searched for the teen, not when the ransom demand came in proving her kidnapping, not when Annie's godfather, the former Sheriff Barkley from five years ago, took over to help. Not even when the ambush at the park happened.

Not even when Helen Murphy died on her picnic blanket during that ambush waiting for her husband to arrive, caught in the cross fire.

It was only after an FBI agent, Jacqueline—Jackie—Ortega, went missing while looking for Annie that people started to suspect something bad was coming.

And when the sheriff and mayor were arrested for orchestrating Annie's kidnapping?

Most knew it was over for normal in Kelby Creek.

For the holdouts, they lost hope when widespread corruption was revealed to have been festering throughout their town for years, while no one had been the wiser.

Five years later and Jones Murphy, a widower since Helen's death, was wiser.

He drove the long way round to his father's home instead of the shortcut through downtown. His father's truck bed was filled with boxes that Jones had dumped into the family storage unit after he'd come back to town with his five-year-old daughter, Bonnie. Coming back to Kelby Creek had been hard enough. Living with his father was proving trickier than he'd originally thought it would be. Ted Murphy was a man who dabbled in multiple hobbies. Hobbies that took up so much space that trips to the storage unit to pack things away and to get his and Bonnie's belongings to the house had become normal since being back.

Not exactly how Jones had expected his homecoming to look. Then again, he hadn't expected to be in Kelby Creek again.

Jones took the extra five minutes of the longer drive to list all the things he had to do in the coming week. Bonnie was starting kindergarten and he had to meet the teachers and principal. His father also needed to start physical therapy for his knee now that the surgery was done. Then there was Bonnie's room. He wanted to paint it Almost Pink, the same color her bedroom had been in every place they'd lived in the last five years. The same color her nursery had been even before she'd been born.

"It's light and warm and feels just rosy enough for a girl who's going to be light and warm, too," Helen had told him, pregnant belly still growing. "And couldn't we all use a little of both?"

Jones tightened his hand on the steering wheel at the memory.

He always tightened when he had to remember that his wife was exactly that.

A memory.

He gritted his teeth and couldn't help but feel an anger in him as he pulled into the drive of his childhood home. Seeing Bonnie would help the anger, but the ache that followed would linger. It always did.

Jones cut the engine and realized the house for sale next door had two vehicles parked in its drive. Both were empty.

All six-five of Jones made his way to and through the front door in seconds. He saw his father's crutches first and his father second. The man and woman sitting across from him on the couch came next.

"I knew he wouldn't be long," his father said to his guests. He looked at Jones. "You have some company, son."

Jones had kept in contact with absolutely no one other than his father after he and Bonnie had left Kelby Creek. But that didn't mean he didn't recognize the man who stood first.

He was older, had grayed and had survived a heart attack during an exceptionally dangerous investigation according to the news a while ago. He'd also been Jones's boss for a short time.

"Brutus Chamblin."

The woman at his side was younger, had a long braid and a severe look. Jones had never met her, but he realized who she was quickly enough.

"Blake Bennet," he added.

She gave a deep nod.

Jones didn't understand why either was at his father's house, but Brutus wasn't a man to beat around the bush.

"You think we can talk outside for a sec?" he asked. "Won't take long."

Jones was ready to say no but his dad was quicker at the draw.

"Best to do it out on the back porch since Bonnie is still napping. Y'all can walk out through the door in the kitchen."

Brutus and Blake didn't wait for an okay from Jones. It put him on edge even more when they did as his dad said and headed to the back porch. Once outside, they faced Jones, but he spoke first.

"When the former and current sheriffs of Kelby Creek come calling, it can't be good."

Brutus, the former and most beloved sheriff in the history of Kelby Creek, cracked a smile. Blake, the current sheriff, had a less-warm reaction.

"We're not here because of trouble or anything sordid," Brutus said. "In fact, we're here in a very opposite capacity." The older man shared a look with Blake. Her posture was already straight, but it seemed to stiffen a bit more as she lifted her chin to meet his gaze.

"No one but us and a few others know this, but I'm leaving my position as sheriff," she began. "My sister passed and I'm taking custody of my niece and nephew, and to make it a little easier on them, I'm moving back to Georgia."

Jones was surprised, but offered his sympathy first.

"I'm sorry for your loss," he said. Blake nodded. She didn't continue, so Jones went with surprise next. He looked to Brutus. "Do you want me to suggest someone for sheriff? You know I haven't been around in years. I mean, I've kept up with the news, but I haven't been on duty with more than half of this new department."

Brutus and Blake shared another look. It should have tipped off Jones.

"We're not asking for suggestions," Blake explained.

Brutus cleared his throat. His smile went serious when he spoke next.

"We're here because we want you to run for sheriff."

Jones blinked a few times because he was sure he hadn't heard him right.

"You've got to be kidding me," he replied.

They were, in fact, not kidding him.

"The job of sheriff is the last piece, Jones," Brutus said. "The department is different, a whole helluva lot different than when you left. It needs a permanent head of the table."

Before he could respond, there was another look between Brutus and Blake.

This time she spoke.

"And we don't just need you to be sheriff. We need you to reinvestigate the Annie McHale kidnapping."

"What do you mean 'reinvestigate'?" Jones asked.

Brutus turned and took a seat at one of the two rocking chairs on the porch. Blake wordlessly followed and stood next to him.

Brutus motioned to the other chair.

"Boy, have we got a story to tell you."

Jones could have said no. He could have asked them to leave. He could have cussed them for even suggesting he ever go back to the department. That he go back and investigate the one case that broke the town, that shattered so many lives and that took Helen's along with it.

Yet, Jones found himself sitting all the same.

"You have one minute."

CASSANDRA WEST DIDN'T typically go to a bar when she was at home. That went doubly so for when she was on the road. Yet, there she was at the hotel bar, a few hours from home, trying not to cry into her drink.

June Smith, her friend and co-teacher, had told her it was more than okay to stay an extra day and just *be*. It was, after all, what should have been her wedding anniversary. It wasn't Cassandra's fault that it coincided with their conference ending.

Yet, there she was, alone at the hotel bar, when she should have been home in her bed crying.

Changing locations wasn't helping her heart. Neither was the wine she was drinking.

It wasn't until a man sat next to her and ordered a beer with the heaviest sigh she'd ever heard that she wondered how the few other patrons viewed her. And it wasn't until that same man turned her way that Cassandra realized her poker face was as disastrous as a spilled can of glitter.

"Been a day, huh?"

Cassandra was glad there was a stool between them. If there hadn't been she would have craned her head all the way back to see the man.

He was tall.

Extremely tall.

And handsome.

Even in the dim bar light, she could see that.

"It has," she agreed amicably.

The man let that lie and Cassandra ran her finger across her glass. The burgeoning tears, thankfully, stayed right where they were. Yet the silence now bothered her. As if the giant man had blown a hole into the darkness and now she had to fill it.

Or maybe that was her personality trying to claw its way back to the surface.

Or maybe it was simply because on any given weekday, she was in a conversation, or twelve, with several small children.

"I don't think people come to hotel bars unless they've been having one," she said after a moment. "A day, that is." She looked around them with a self-deprecating smile. "Or maybe they're tired from whatever work conference or travel they're doing and drinking from the minifridge is just too expensive."

The man smirked at that statement.

"Then there's how expensive room service is," he said. "I took one look at how much a sandwich ran for and decided it was time to close the menu."

Cassandra agreed.

"I was lucky enough to get a food allowance for my work thing and it still was ridiculous. My coworkers and I spent one night at McDonald's to save some money."

It was a pleasant, nothing conversation.

But it felt nice.

"Are you here for work?" she asked, surprising herself. "I heard there was an accountants' type of get-together starting tomorrow."

The man didn't look like an accountant, but sometimes she was told she didn't look like an elementary school teacher. Mostly because when she didn't have to be at school, her outfits ran more formal. Sometimes it was a nice change of pace to wear a pencil skirt versus a sundress with a cardigan that had rainbow patches all over it.

"I am but I'm not," the man answered. The bartender delivered his drink. He explained before she could decide if she was going to follow up with that. "I'm trying to decide if I should take a job or not. To do that I decided to give myself some time to think without distractions. Hence, getting a hotel room even though I have a perfectly good home I could be at."

"According to my friend, sometimes you just need somewhere you can just be and usually that's easier at a place like this."

The man chuckled.

"I guess it makes sense. I'll have to remind myself of that, though, when the bill comes in." He stretched out his hand to her. "I'm Jones."

Cassandra wished she had more time to marvel at how large his hand was around hers as she shook it. Instead, she was quick.

"Cassandra—a woman with a friend who sounds like a fortune-cookie writer."

He laughed again. This time, though, his gaze seemed to linger on her.

It made something in Cassandra shift.

It also brought on a slight blush.

She tried to distract herself from it.

"So this job—what was your gut reaction to the offer? Or are you a pro-and-con-list kind of guy instead of only listening to your instincts?"

Jones ran a thumb across his jaw and sighed again.

"Well, the problem is I'm an instincts guy who still likes making lists. My gut reaction was to turn the job down but also to take it. My list had the same amount of pros and cons."

"Which means as of right now you should and shouldn't take it."

He nodded.

Cassandra swiveled in her seat so she could face him. She thought about his predicament for a little bit, trying to stay respectful of his privacy. To an extent.

"Have you ever seen the show *Friends*?"

The question seemed to catch the man off guard. He answered all the same.

"Some of it as reruns, but I couldn't name the characters off even with a gun to my head."

Cassandra smiled.

"Well, there's something one of the characters does to try and figure out how they're really feeling. It's a game. I ask quick questions and you give quick answers. No time to pause and think. Just answer. It might help you push you over your indecision?"

Jones made a face, but then turned on his stool so he was finally open to her.

"At this point what would it hurt to try?"

Cassandra put down her drink and used her hands,

palms up, for each option. Given her profession of dealing with little kids all of the time, she was always using
her hands when she spoke.

"Ready?"

Jones smiled. "Ready."

Cassandra didn't skip a beat. "Red or blue?" she
started.

"Blue," he said immediately.

"Cats or dogs?"

"Dogs."

"The moon landing was faked, yes or no?"

"No."

"Alabama or Auburn?"

"Alabama."

"Beer or whiskey?"

"Beer."

"Rain or shine?"

"Rain."

"Do you want this job, yes or no?"

"Yes."

The answer was as quick as the rest, if not quicker.

Cassandra watched as Jones's eyes widened. Then
his expression melted into an easy smile.

She joined in.

"I don't know about your pro-and-con list but I think
your instincts want you to take the job," she said. "But
that's just my opinion and, I should note, I don't even
know what job it was you were offered, so I can't take
responsibility if you take it and it doesn't work out."

Jones was back to smirking.

"I'm not about to blame someone who just ended

my day-long turmoil of indecision." He took a sip of his drink. Cassandra mirrored him. She half expected them to slip back into silence, but Jones didn't let them. "In fact, maybe I can repay you by buying you dinner? Someplace that's more reasonably priced than the mini-fridge, of course."

Cassandra didn't normally drink at unfamiliar bars. Even less so did she accept dinner invites from men she met in them.

Yet…there was something about the man that stuck.

Or maybe your heart hurts and he's managed to make you forget that for a few minutes.

Cassandra wasn't sure what her reasons were for saying yes, but she did.

Had she known that their dinner would turn into one amazing night spent back in her room, she might have hesitated.

But, in the moment, all she said was "I won't say no to that."

Chapter One

Ray Cooke was two steps from the side of a bridge that if he fell from, would surely make his bad day that much worse.

Jones saw the man as he got out of his father's truck, but he let his new chief deputy walk up to him before he made his way to Ray's side.

"What's he going on about?" Jones asked his right-hand man.

Carlos Park had been a part of the Dawn County Sheriff's Department since before The Flood, a series of events that started with Annie McHale's kidnapping and snowballed into a corruption case involving her godfather, Sheriff Barkley, and the mayor, both of whom had played a major role in the crime. It was why trust had been so low in town every day since, but people like Carlos and his team were trying to earn it back. If Carlos stayed long enough, Jones suspected he'd be the next sheriff down the road. Now he looked close to rolling his eyes at good ol' Ray Cooke, one of their frequent flyers at the jail.

"He's drunk as a skunk and talking about his lady

again," Carlos said with a heavy dose of "same song and dance" in his tone. "She went off with Trevor, he thinks, and Ray's trying to take out his frustration by yelling at any and all cars driving through. Lucky for him it's piss early and the only car he yelled at was Millie's, and she knows how to handle herself."

It had been seven months since Jones had been asked to run for sheriff. He'd done that, been elected and had those months to get his feet wet, so to speak.

Now he knew that Millie was the wife of their lead detective, Foster Lovett, and given their history, she could, in fact, hold her own. Just as he now knew that Ray Cooke didn't listen to reason when he was being belligerent. He only responded to something bigger and scarier than him.

"It's just like scaring a bear off the trail by making yourself seem larger and louder," Kathryn Juliet, one of their detectives, had instructed when Jones had been on his way to his first Ray Cooke experience. "Last time Howie went, she actually waved her arms a little to make herself seem bigger. It worked."

Jones wasn't about to wave his arms. He didn't have to.

Ray might have been six feet tall, but Jones was well over that.

"All right, you head on to the department. I got this," Jones said to Carlos at his cruiser.

"How about I just make the first call I need to make today in my car," Carlos offered instead. "Ray might be harmless but better safe than sorry."

Before The Flood, Jones might have shooed the man

away without a second thought, but he no longer trusted his gut on who was or wasn't harmless anymore. He'd made that mistake before with trusting Sheriff Barkley and everyone else who had become a part of the corruption. That was even accounting for Annie McHale's specific investigation, something Jones was itching to get back to instead of dealing with Ray and his women troubles.

"All right," Jones conceded. "This won't take but a minute."

Ray Cooke was standing on the road side of the bridge's concrete railing. Though there was nothing too mighty about the structure. It was just made to keep cars off the creek water that rose too high in the rain. Given it was more of a trickle than a creek beneath the bridge, it wasn't all that worrisome if Ray tried to flee over its edge. He'd drop maybe four feet, get a little wet and limp along until they got him.

Maybe that's why he'd picked this bridge and not one of the others in town that had a good amount of water beneath them.

Ray liked pretending he had control, that he had options.

He didn't. At least, none of them good.

Jones approached the man and looped his thumbs between his belt and pants. Ray took a moment to really look at Jones before he went on the defensive, putting his arms across his chest and holding his chin high.

"Well, look who got the sheriff out to see him," Ray sneered. "Must be rating pretty high to get that kinda treatment."

Jones held in his sigh.

"Morning, Ray," he greeted. "Been a minute."

Ray was a younger man who looked like he'd probably been a good quarterback in high school. Square shoulders, wide arms, could run at a decent clip. Wasn't too big, wasn't too thin. But after his glory days were over, he'd softened for whatever reason.

He looked like he was "hunched against the wind," as Jones's dad liked to say.

But troubles or no, Ray couldn't keep doing what he was doing. One day he was going to cause trouble he couldn't take back and that was something that no one wanted.

Ray wasn't done sneering. He made a show of looking Jones up and down.

"There wasn't no need for you to come on out." He nodded to Carlos's cruiser. "No need for any of you. I wasn't doing nothing."

"You were barking at cars, Ray," Jones responded. "That's not nothing, especially when you follow it up by running into the road. Someone could have been hurt, or worse, you included."

Ray scoffed, shook his head enough to cross his eyes a moment and set his jaw like a man who wasn't going to make the next few minutes easy.

"No one can take a joke in this town. That's all it was. Me being funny. But *no*, ain't you or anyone at that box of nothings going to see that." He pointed out at Jones but his eyes went to the sheriff's star on his breast pocket. "That badge don't mean a thing. Just something to keep crumbs off of your shirt."

Jones kept his relaxed stance. This was tame talk compared to some other verbal altercations he'd had during his career before The Flood.

"It also looks nice in pictures," Jones said with a small smile. "Not to mention makes me responsible for keeping everyone as safe as I can. So why don't you let me give you a ride home and you can sleep off last night there?"

Because of his experiences with Ray in the last few months, Jones expected the man to hesitate before relenting with a nod. But, for whatever reason, this Monday morning, Ray was proud.

He stuck out his chest and gave Jones a stare that would have stung had Ray been serious. When he spoke it was snake-in-the-grass deceptive.

"A badge didn't help save your wife—what makes you think this one can save any of us?"

Jones had nerves of steel, body strength near it and could shut his mouth like a vault when needed.

But Ray's pride and the words that followed had taken a bite out of Jones. A surprisingly harsh one.

Which made him want to bite right on back.

Jones unhooked his thumbs from his belt and slowly started toward the smaller man.

And Ray *was* small.

Lightweight in body, heavyweight in mind.

He wasn't so sure of his words the closer Jones got. That much was clear.

"You get two options, Ray Cooke," Jones growled. "You either call the one taxi in this whole town and get going in it, or you accept my more-than-nice offer to give you a ride and you shut your mouth until I drop you at your front door. Do you understand?"

Ray had to raise his chin to keep eye contact. He'd gone awfully still for a man keen on slinging pointed comments.

Jones leaned into the quiet.

"Do you understand me?" he repeated. "Or do I need to rephrase the options?"

Ray finally broke.

His eyes hit the ground, his arms went limp at his sides.

"Could you call me up the cab? I got enough to get home."

Jones took a moment but nodded into his rising anger. He called the only transportation that ran in town and, when the driver heard it was the sheriff, he arrived promptly.

The anger was still there as Jones watched Ray get in.

It was still there when the taillights disappeared in the distance.

It would probably be there all day, if Jones was being honest with himself.

Mostly, because it was true.

"You good?" Carlos asked with genuine concern. That concern turned to abject sympathy. "Ray has a way of getting under the skin sometimes. No matter what he says, it's just coming from a place of regret from his own life choices. Once, my girl—my friend Amanda—overheard him say at the bar that he wishes he'd never gotten back together with Lottie the first time. Said he should have left to go to college instead. Left all the bad behind."

Jones sighed, pushing that anger in him far enough away to deal with later.

"I still wish he wouldn't bark at cars, though."

Carlos agreed.

"I'm heading back to the department now to talk to Kenneth about the cold-case task force's progress on another cold case. Last night, Lily—Detective Howard, I mean—and Kenneth were pretty dang close to figuring something out. I don't think they knew what, but I've seen them almost work miracles, so I bet they've got something now. You heading there or working out-of-office today?"

Jones had a folder in his truck, beneath the passenger seat. He had copies of it at work, but it was there so he could disappear into it no matter where he was.

Today he wanted to do it around town and not behind his desk.

"I have to check up on some things. Then I'll be back in."

Carlos nodded. He might have been second-in-command, but he didn't need a play-by-play on what Jones was doing. He knew, even if he didn't know the hourly details of it.

"Good luck, Sheriff."

Jones's mind stuck on the title *Sheriff.* It still felt off to him. A shoe that fit but only with the perfect sock.

He didn't mind it but he didn't love it yet, either.

"You, too."

Jones watched Carlos drive off. He didn't immediately follow.

Fall was being kind to Kelby Creek. Cool enough for him to keep his jacket handy, not cold enough to keep his heavy one zipped up. It also had the sky dancing between hazy, orange and clear. The rain would come, sure, but the menace behind their summer storms had lessened.

There was a calmness in fall.

That calm only lasted a few moments in Jones's chest.

He needed to decide where to go next.

The McHale Manor, or to talk to the gardener next door.

Maybe you should play the question game, he thought with an equal level of seriousness and amusement.

It had, after all, worked out for him last time.

He'd run for sheriff and won.

He'd found a new purpose in an old pain.

He'd spent the night with a beautiful woman.

The same woman who had suggested they treat their time together as something wonderful but something brief.

"Some things are beautiful because they end," she'd said. "Let's keep this beautiful."

Jones had been surprised at the suggestion, but maybe not so much at his agreeing to it.

Maybe it was the way she'd said it, or maybe she'd been right.

Sometimes it was better to end things the right way than have them ended for you.

Still, as Jones hopped into his truck and took in the autumn sky one more time, he couldn't help his mind going back to the memory of her laugh, her smile, the way he'd forgotten for a while that he had a hole in him.

Then Jones shook his head and turned over the engine.

Best not to lose sleep over someone he'd likely never see again.

CASSANDRA WAS STARING down the barrel of a paper-towel roll and right into the eye of Keith McGibbon. She was tense; he was smiling. She could move, run, or at the very least hit the cardboard away, but in her experience that would only set off Keith.

And if she'd learned anything in the last three months, it was that you didn't openly antagonize a kindergartener who had a handful of glitter balled up in his hand.

"Let's take a calming breath, Keith," she said.

Keith had turned six over the weekend, and today they'd thrown him a little party at lunch. An hour later, the candy from the festivities was obviously still spiking his energy level and exhausting hers.

And tricky.

Keith was going through a phase where he pretended to be a pirate at every turn. Normally it was harmless, but somehow he'd found his way to the glitter stash and it was Cassandra who would pay the price if she didn't get through to him.

"Pirates don't throw glitter," she added matter-of-factly. "It goes against their code."

Keith lowered his pretend periscope.

"The pirate code?"

Cassandra didn't break eye contact.

"Yes, sir! Pirates have a code, one they always live by," she said. "Throwing glitter at people goes against that because once glitter gets into something it doesn't get out. That's why glitter is only ever used in art class and for crafting."

Keith seemed to consider that.

Behind him at one of the learning stations, her colleague, June, eyed the interaction with clear concern. And very apparent relief that it wasn't her. They, like most kindergarten teachers, had a running joke about how powerfully awful glitter was. No matter how far you stayed away from it, it followed you home, got into your best clothes and somehow, sometimes could be found in your hair even if you hadn't been around a jar of it in days.

If Keith decided to forsake her last-second addition to the imaginary pirate code, Cassandra was sure she'd be sporting that glitter until the day she retired.

Luckily, though, Keith's loyalty to his pirate lifestyle won out. Slowly he lifted his hand to her, palm up.

Cassandra was fast. She gently guided it and him to the trash can by the classroom door.

"The pirates thank you," she told him as the devil dust showered down into the plastic bag.

Once the threat was gone, Keith returned to his station under the extra watchful eye of June. Cassandra went back to her independent-play kids and, before she knew it, the clock hit two thirty.

"I'll take the kids to car pool since I almost cost you a nice dress," June said with a laugh after the class had lined up. Her eyes flitted down. "Plus, you have to be a little tired. You've been on your feet all day."

Cassandra rolled her eyes.

"The offer to take the kids, I'll accept. Thinking I can't stand an extra half hour just because I have some added weight, I'll deny."

June laughed and Cassandra smiled at the chorus of goodbyes from their students.

It wasn't until all were out of sight that Cassandra did take a seat behind her desk. She was tired, but it had nothing to do with standing all day and everything to do with the protruding belly that was taking up room beneath her maternity dress.

"'You probably won't show that much until closer to your due date,'" she mockingly said to herself, repeating her doctor's words. "'Since this is your first baby and all.'"

Cassandra snorted.

Even at six and a half months, she was undeniably round and pregnant.

Kelby Creek Elementary went from chaos to quiet as the clock inched past three. June returned after carpool duty and collected her things before saying goodbye. Cassandra was going through her lesson plan and the next day's activities when a custodial worker moved through their classroom, and on to the rest of the kindergarten wing of the school. Then the quiet seemed loud, and Cassandra realized it was time to go.

She loaded her purse with things she didn't need and

made her way to the heart of the school. Instead of cutting to her left to go out to the car-pool pickup and the front doors, though, she paused by the wall of windows that showed the playground in the back.

Mrs. Letterman, the oldest on staff at Kelby Creek Elementary, looked defeated next to the jungle gym. She was on extended day duty. Today there were only two kids left.

Cassandra sighed when she saw Keith among the two. She nixed her plan to go home and walked out to Mrs. Letterman with a smile.

"These two the only ones left?"

Mrs. Letterman nodded.

Keith looked up and the girl he was playing with turned. She wasn't Cassandra's student, but she knew her name was Bonnie. Her dark curls were as wild as her personality. Which was probably why Mrs. Letterman looked particularly tired.

She'd been assigned extended day with two of the most energetic kindergarteners this side of the Mississippi.

Cassandra laughed as Bonnie gave a war cry that was instantly repeated by Keith.

"How about I take over and you head out?" Cassandra offered to Mrs. Letterman. Before the older woman could politely refuse, Cassandra lifted her hand in a stop motion. "Let me do this before my maternity leave sneaks up on us and leaves everyone one teacher down. I really don't mind."

Mrs. Letterman only hesitated a little.

"Keith said his grown-up runs late sometimes and

Bonnie's grandfather called and said he was having car trouble, but her dad is going to be here any minute. Coach Rich is in his office still. Let him know when you head out."

Mrs. Letterman left like the world was chasing her. Quite deceptive for her age.

Cassandra set down her bag, then put one hand on her belly and one on the bar closest to her on the gym. Keith was grinning from ear-to-ear at her.

"We're walking the planks," he told her, pride in his voice. "Bonnie said she has a wooden leg."

"That must make swimming a bit harder, huh?" Cassandra asked Bonnie, who was standing next to the jungle gym and not beneath it like her crew member.

But her attention wasn't on Cassandra. It wasn't on Keith, either.

Instead, Bonnie was wide-eyed, her focus past both of them and in the direction of the fence that faced the faculty parking lot, where the buses turned around after picking up and dropping off kids. It was also where parents could sign out their kids from extended day.

Yet, when Cassandra turned, she didn't recognize the man at the gate.

Keith was only allowed to be picked up by his foster mom and social worker, both women. Definitely not the man.

Cassandra directed her question to Bonnie, but didn't break eye contact with the stranger.

"Bonnie, is that your dad?"

Bonnie took a small step back.

The man went through the gate, a hundred or so yards away from them.

"No." Bonnie's voice had gone as quiet as the playground around them.

The hair on the back of Cassandra's neck stood.

She kept her voice low when she spoke next.

"Keith, come grab my hand."

Bless the boy—he listened. A second later his sticky hand was in hers.

The man seemed to get faster at the move. He wasn't smiling. Not even a little.

"Bonnie," Cassandra continued, "I need you to run as fast as you can to the doors. Right *now*."

Bless Bonnie—she was just as good a listener.

Chapter Two

The man was tall and slender. Unflinching.

His clothes were normal in their everyday appearance—a button-up shirt and jeans. He had golden hair that curled a little and a few creases along his forehead that made it hard for her to place his age. If there was a weapon on him, it was hidden. And, if there was a reason he gave chase the moment Cassandra ran with the children, he didn't voice it.

No "Hey, sorry I startled y'all. This is just a big ol' misunderstanding."

No "It's okay. I'm here for a valid reason that has nothing to do with ill intent."

The man was as quiet as a statue.

One that would have no doubt reached them had Cassandra not thrown the lock on the door as soon as the three of them were through.

The man slammed into it, but didn't make a noise when the door didn't give.

"This is an emergency," Bonnie said from behind Cassandra. "We need to call my dad!"

Cassandra pictured her phone in the bottom of her

purse. The same purse she'd left on the ground next to the jungle gym. Had she known some strange man would be running after them, Cassandra wouldn't have put it down at all.

"The front office has a phone we can—"

Cassandra's attempt at a quick plan and providing reassurance was dashed. The man took two steps back and squatted. He was as quick at scooping up one of the painted rocks as he was at rearing back and throwing it.

Cassandra jumped back, taking Keith and pushing Bonnie with her, just as the rock collided with the glass top of the door.

The pumpkin shape on the rock was cute.

The way the glass turned into a spiderweb of cracks made her stomach drop below her feet.

"Come on!"

Cassandra pulled the kids toward the center of the school. Several hallways fed into the main hub before branching off into the front end, where the office, cafeteria and front pickup area were. She had every intention of going to the office, hoping Mrs. Letterman had dallied and could call for help ASAP, but the sickening sound of glass shattering made her plan of getting to a phone go off the rails.

When the back door made an awful noise opening over the broken glass, Cassandra went with a plan that would hopefully get them to some doors that weren't so easily broken into.

She took a turn that almost made Keith lose his footing and soon all three were in the elementary school's library.

"Be quiet," she whispered to the kids.

To their utter credit, they kept on listening to her, even when she took them right into the stacks.

Kelby Creek Elementary's library wasn't the biggest space in the school, but it was mighty all its own. Seven rows of bookcases created four long aisles that ended at a square of open space at the back corner. Cassandra ushered both children toward that corner, mind already on the door that said Employees Only behind it. That door led to the storage room that connected to the back of the teachers' lounge. For as long as Cassandra had been teaching at the school, neither the storage room nor its connecting door had been locked.

But the teacher's lounge *could* be locked when inside.

It didn't have a landline but if she could make sure the children were safe inside, Cassandra could bolt to the office and hope it was open so she could make a call. Each classroom had a landline, but everyone locked up before they left for the day.

Where was the custodian?

Had she already left?

What about Coach Rich?

There was a clattering behind them.

The door flung open.

Cassandra took the kids along to the right and stopped between two of the aisles. Bonnie was fastened to her back, Keith to her front. She didn't want to, but Cassandra put her hand over the boy's mouth. He was a talker when the going was good; she didn't know how he would be in a situation like this.

Footfalls moved outside of the shelves. The man was searching the desk and the reader area of the room first.

It was a small blessing.

One that gave Cassandra hope.

She tapped Bonnie's arm and slowly slid her hand off Keith's mouth. Cassandra took both of them by the hand again and kept going to her earlier destination.

The Employees Only sign was a beacon of light.

Keith and Bonnie were wide-eyed as the door opened. Everyone was blessedly quiet and still, the door included.

Cassandra pushed the kids inside and shut the door behind them with more concentration than she'd ever had. It was a soft close.

"Keep going," she whispered to the children, nodding toward the other side of the room.

For as long as she lived, Cassandra would never forget how beautifully calm the two were. Quiet but terrified, and following her instructions while someone came after them. Most adults would have already folded.

Not them.

They were pirates.

Bonnie made it to the next door first. Her hands went around the knob as Cassandra was already mentally slamming the door behind them and looking it tight. Yet, when Bonnie turned nothing happened.

Cassandra's blood went cold. Bonnie tried again before she could get there. The door still wasn't opening.

Cassandra moved her aside and hoped the six-year-old had been clumsy at the attempt.

But, she hadn't.

The door that was never locked was locked.

"What do we do?" Keith's voice broke into the quiet.

Cassandra touched her belly, trying to think of a back-up plan. She looked around the room with new, terrified eyes.

The storage room wasn't the only one in the school and wasn't at all big. There was nowhere to hide and not enough space to get around someone standing in the doorway.

Did the man have a weapon?

Would he try to hurt them?

Take them?

Why was he here?

What could he want?

Cassandra didn't have time to do anything but cycle through her questions in a hurried mess.

The door they'd come in from opened.

Cassandra whirled around and pushed Keith behind her in the process. The man paused his strides to take in the scene.

No one spoke for a moment.

Cassandra then broke the quiet.

"Leave them here and I'll go with you," she said, voice even and firm. It surprised even herself.

Not as much as the man's response, though.

He didn't smile but he certainly didn't frown.

"No," he said. "I don't want you."

That was it.

Those were the magic words.

The ice in Cassandra's veins went to boiling quick.

The man wanted the kids.

The man was about to get her.

Cassandra went into full guardian mode. She let go of the children's hands and was standing still one second, and running at the man the next.

The element of surprise proved useful.

He took a few steps back and out the doorway.

Cassandra didn't stop. She threw her hands out and pushed into his chest as hard as she could.

The man yelled out, stumbling at the contact.

Cassandra kept the attack going.

She grabbed two fistfuls of his shirt and tried to sling him into the closest bookshelf.

The move gave her a half of what she wanted.

He didn't hit the shelf, but he did fall.

"Bonnie! Keith! Run!"

Whatever calm Cassandra had been possessing turned into a bark of a demand. But, again, the kids listened.

Bonnie ran out of the storage room pulling Keith along with her as Cassandra grabbed for the closest book from a shelf. Cassandra felt the whoosh of air as they went past her.

They weren't the only ones who were fast.

The man got up to his feet quickly.

Cassandra hit him in the face with an early readers chapter book.

It wasn't hard enough for him to go down again, but it was hard enough to tick him off. He made an awful noise and lunged forward.

Cassandra yelled in surprise and got a taste of her

own medicine. He hit her shoulders hard, but before she could fall, one of his hands went to her hair.

She yelled out again as pain lit up her scalp. On reflex, she went to grab his wrist but he yanked her downward. With one hand going to cradle her stomach, she managed to hit the ground with her hip instead.

The man released his hold but Cassandra saw his eyes.

He was going to hurt her, and now that she was on the ground beneath him, all he had to do was hit or kick her and he would do just that.

Cassandra moved her arm over her stomach and readied to try and defend herself as best she could, when something happened that made both of them jump.

The fire alarm went off.

And then a book hit the man's hip.

Cassandra turned just as another book was launched through the air.

Keith was already reaching for another from the shelf closest.

"Run," Cassandra yelled out, but all Keith did was try and hit the man again.

And the man didn't appreciate it one bit.

He went for Keith.

Cassandra kicked out but missed his feet.

She yelled out to the boy to run again, but Keith froze. Cassandra's adrenaline was nothing but a flood raging through her body.

She scrambled to her feet just as the man grabbed Keith.

The boy yelled, and so did Cassandra.

She needed to end the fight.
She needed to stop the man.
Now.

JONES LEFT THE sheriff's department cussing, but managed not to speed on his way to the elementary school. It wasn't his dad's fault that his truck's engine had up and died. It also wasn't the first time Bonnie had gone to extended day when plans had changed at the last minute. Still, Jones hated the idea of Bonnie looking out for her grandpa and instead getting shuffled to the playground to wait when he didn't come.

It's why Jones wanted to get there fast.

Waiting for someone you love and them not showing up hurt, even when you knew the reason behind it.

So Jones parked in the school lot and jumped out, still wearing his badge and his holster, with his service weapon tucked inside. His feet hit the asphalt and then the sidewalk to the playground gate before he thought about putting the weapon in the car. But that thought stalled as quick as spit when Jones realized he was staring out at an empty playground.

Well, not completely.

The jungle gym, Bonnie's favorite piece of equipment, was unoccupied in the middle of the space. Next to it was a bag.

Not just any bag—it was a purse on the ground.

Jones looked back at the parking lot. Three cars. He burned all three into memory and opened the gate.

No one called out to him as he moved across the grass and sand to the purse. One glance down showed an adult-size shoe print and at least two pairs of kids' feet. They trailed up to the doors leading back into the school.

Jones felt adrenaline spike and rage through his system as he looked at those doors.

One was shut.

The other had its glass absolutely shattered.

Jones went for his phone at his hip, his other hand hovering over his gun. Before he could move, something else made the world around him take on a more menacing feel.

The fire alarm started blaring through the school.

He threw open the back door and crunched his way over the broken glass into the hallway.

It was as eerie as it was concerning.

There was no one around. Just the strobe lights of the alarm and its loud warning.

Jones put his hand on the butt of his gun.

He almost drew it when a sudden burst of movement caught his eye deeper in the school.

His heart burst with relief when he saw that it was a little girl.

His little girl.

"Bonnie!"

Chapter Three

With wild dark hair and eyes that were exactly her mother's, Bonnie locked in on him and he knew in an instant that something *was* terribly wrong.

She was terrified.

"Dad," she yelled out, running full speed at him.

However, instead of colliding into him, she skidded to a stop a foot away.

Her hands were so small as they waved backward and then pointed.

"There's a man hurting Miss West!"

Her voice was small but confident.

Jones believed her in an instant.

"Just one man?" Jones took his cell phone out and handed it to her as Bonnie nodded. "Call 911 and tell them where we are and we need help. Tell them your name. Can you do that?"

Jones knew Bonnie could. He'd done several emergency drills with her from toddler age to the present. He knew how dangerous the world was and he'd wanted to make sure Bonnie was as prepared as a small child could be, including how to use any phone to call for help.

"Yeah, I can," she exclaimed.

Jones couldn't take her with him. It was too risky. They'd done drills similar to this before. Hiding when needed, running when needed too. Jones also knew the rough layout of the school. He pointed in the direction of the older students' bathrooms.

"Go hide in one of the bathroom stalls and do it," Jones ordered. "Be quiet until I come back."

Jones watched his daughter nod and then was off to where she'd pointed.

He might not know what the situation was, who Miss West was, or why the man was causing trouble, but Jones knew one thing for sure.

He was about to put a stop to it right now.

He heard noises from an open door, the sounds of scuffling and worse. Jones hadn't been in the elementary library before, but he didn't need a breakdown of the layout to see what needed to happen as soon as he rushed inside.

"Let go!"

There was a man and woman in between two of the bookshelves near the back of the room. Jones couldn't see either of their faces because of their positions, but he could make out that the man had his arms around a boy between them.

And, while Bonnie was only six, Jones trusted his daughter's plea.

Miss West was being attacked by the man.

Which meant the man was the problem.

Jones kept the element of surprise as he closed the gap between him and the fighting. Miss West surely wasn't making the man's life easier. She heaved a book through the air and hit his shoulder. Then she threw out a punch that didn't land, though it did make the man take a step back to avoid it.

The boy in his arms didn't stick to the movement. He flailed out and toward the teacher just as she grabbed at his shirt. The whole exchange took less than thirty seconds, but it was just enough time to give Jones the perfect lead-in.

He focused solely on the man and bellowed out.

"Sheriff's department—stop where you are!"

The man spun around. His eyes were wide with surprise and panic. He was tall but he wasn't Jones tall, and the best he could guess, the man hadn't counted on him showing up. Jones started to repeat himself but the man's apparent fight response turned to flight just as quickly.

He lunged forward and directly at the boy and teacher, but instead of grabbing for them, he pushed them down and ran past them as they hit the floor.

"You okay?" Jones yelled out to them, already moving.

He saw the woman nod out of his peripheral vision as he sped up.

It was clear that the man hadn't been in the library before, either. He ran clumsily and turned into a dead end made up of bookshelves.

"Stop and put your hands up right now," Jones said, blocking his escape. He went to tap his badge but the man decided to be bold again.

Instead of putting his hands up in surrender, the intruder turned and pushed the bookshelf with all that he had. And, since they were in a public school and not some high-end library, that bookshelf did a mighty fine job of giving up.

Books hit the floor before the metal made it over onto the gray, rug-covered tile.

It was a nasty noise. The boy behind him in the stacks yelled. His attacker scurried over the fallen bookshelf. It opened up his escape route to the study side of the library.

Well, at least it gave him the illusion that he had a chance to leave.

"All right," Jones growled out. "We're not going to keep doing this."

He backtracked through the stacks and used his long strides to his advantage. The culprit made it to the door a second after Jones.

It was then, in the man's infinite wisdom, that he tried to go back to fighting.

He balled his fist and swung out hard. Had Jones been a smaller man, the hit might have landed with some heft.

Instead, it gave Jones the opening he needed to dole out his own punishment.

The man yelled out as Jones leveled him with a solid hit along his jaw.

He went slack right after.

Jones said a little cuss under his breath as he pulled his pair of cuffs from the back of his belt. It was easy work securing them on the man's wrists, and even easier work to confirm he was unconscious due to the punch.

That hadn't been Jones's intent, but given where they were and what the man had seemingly been up to, maybe it was best he take a little time-out.

Finally, when Jones was sure the threat was neutralized, he was able to really check on the boy and Miss West.

Both had made their way to their feet and both were staring at him with wide eyes.

He looked to the boy first. He was crying, but there were no obvious wounds. He was scared but not hurt. Miss West had her hands on his shoulders, steadying him. It seemed the only reason he might not have been completely breaking down. That, and shock.

Jones was relieved.

Then he was abruptly shocked himself.

For the first time since coming into the library, Jones was able to look at Miss West. *Really* look. Not a passing, calculated glance to get the bare facts.

A true *look* at her.

She might not have been Bonnie's teacher, but Jones absolutely knew her.

"Cassandra?"

The woman he thought about every time he sat down behind his desk or caught his badge's reflection in the mirror.

The woman who had helped him decide on a different future than the one he was planning.

The woman he'd spent one hell of a night with before they'd agreed to part ways with no more than the fond memories they'd shared.

That decision he'd often regretted in the last several months, but they'd only exchanged first names.

But now, there she was.

Cassandra West, apparently.

Teacher at his daughter's school.

And she was, without a doubt, just as surprised to see him.

"Jones?" she asked.

He might have answered—or asked several questions all at once—had the boy not moved aside so he could turn to see Cassandra better. But he did and that's when Jones saw all of her.

Not only was Cassandra in Kelby Creek, at his daughter's school, and standing no more than a few feet from him, but she was also pregnant.

"Dad?" All thoughts screamed to a halt as Bonnie's voice yelled out from behind him. "Can I come in now?"

Jones cut eye contact with Cassandra and found his little girl standing uncertainly in the doorway. Her gaze had fallen to the man beneath him.

It sobered him.

It didn't matter right now that Cassandra was in Kelby Creek.

It only mattered why the man was.

BONNIE RAN IN and there wasn't much time between her coming back into the library and another man of the law running in, too.

Marco Rossi, a deputy sheriff, came in quickly with his badge, looking concerned. He took in the scene with grave attention. He focused on Jones next.

"What do you need from me, Sheriff?"

Cassandra, who believed herself to be in some kind of shock, was shaken a little at that revelation. Just as she had been to hear Bonnie call Jones "Dad."

Jones wasn't just in Kelby Creek, he was the sheriff of it.

Before Cassandra could come to terms with that realization, the man who had attacked them started to stir. Keith went back to her side in a flash. Bonnie backtracked to Cassandra, too, taking one of her hands. Cassandra had the other one on her stomach.

"Let's get him out of here," Jones answered after a quick look at Bonnie, her and Keith. "Your cruiser outside, Rossi?"

Marco shook his head.

"We just came from car pool here about twenty minutes ago," he said. "All I had time to do was drop off the kids and turn back around. Sterling's close though. He should be here any second."

Jones nodded and hoisted the man up. His head lolled to the side, but his feet found the ground easily enough. Bonnie tightened her hold on Cassandra's hand. It was like her father felt her anxiety flare. His focus went to her.

"Bonnie, you and your friend stay here with Miss West and Deputy Rossi here. I'll be back in a jiffy."

Marco took the order with a nod, and Bonnie said okay. Cassandra, still feeling like she was in some bizarre dream, took an uncertain step forward.

"Jones… I mean, Sheriff?" she said.

Jones's perfect warm eyes—the same eyes she'd

stared into longingly during their one night together—
met hers and Cassandra almost became speechless.

After their time together at the hotel, Cassandra had
wished they hadn't made the rule of just being passing
ships in the night. Sure, she wasn't looking for a relationship and it seemed the man had had a lot on his
mind with not a lot of room for any other thoughts or
people. Yet, when Cassandra had made it home to her
bed the next night, she'd looked at the pillow next to
her and wished Jones had been there.

If not kissing, talking, and even if not talking, just
being there.

Because that's what their time together had been like.
Brief but poignant. Small talk that felt whole. Intimacy
even without the details of their lives. Details that would
have complicated their already complicated lives.

Details that would have let them know they were
headed home to the same exact zip code.

But that night of longing had turned into regret,
anger and then acceptance that the man named Jones
might never cross her path again. That her luck in love
and life would never be that good.

Then, to prove to her that nothing worked out the
way she ever planned, she'd realized her period hadn't
shown.

When she found out that she was pregnant and Jones
was the only man she'd been with since Ryan?

Well, she'd fallen right out of acceptance and gone
to anger and grief.

She'd always wanted kids but she'd never thought

she'd be a single parent. And what about what Jones wanted?

That thought had haunted her as the months went by and her stomach, and their baby, grew.

Only June knew who the father was, and even so she hadn't known him, just the name.

"You could hire a private eye to try and find him," June had suggested once she'd made it to her third trimester. "You know, see who he really is before you tell him you're expecting. Maybe even wait until Kiddo is born to feel him out in person before you bring him into your lives."

It had been good advice Cassandra had often thought about taking.

Yet, every time she did, she'd think of Ryan.

She'd think of the wedding she never had.

She'd think of her luck.

Then she'd decide to think about it all again later.

But, now?

Now that Jones was in front of her?

Now that she saw his badge?

It didn't feel real.

So Cassandra stayed in the present.

She pushed back her shoulders and made sure her voice was strong and even, so as not to frighten the children anymore.

"Keith's grown-ups might show up," she said. "Lila Shaw or Renee Parr. Coach Rich might also be in the gym still, but I'm not sure. Other than that the school should be empty."

Jones, in all of his massive glory, nodded.

Then it was like he put on a mask. Or, really, a face of concentration unlike any Cassandra had seen him wear during their night of passion as strangers in a hotel room.

"I'll keep a lookout," he told her. "Thanks."

Cassandra nodded.

It felt wholly inadequate.

"No problem."

She watched him go, pulling the unknown man along with him. Marco, as directed, stayed. Keith pressed his body weight into Cassandra's leg. Bonnie kept Cassandra's hand.

She contemplated how strange life was, to be holding the sheriff's daughter's hand while also carrying his son.

Chapter Four

There was a lot going on, but almost none of it provided Jones with any answers that made a whole lot of sense.

"It takes some stones to go after children on the playground," Carlos said to Jones as they watched a cruiser leaving the school. "I never thought Bill a man to do anything like that."

Jones and Kelby Creek transplant Marco hadn't recognized Bill Burrows, the man who'd had the absolute gall to chase Jones's daughter, but Carlos and Sterling had been quick to identify him. Bill had gone to school with Sterling when they were young. He currently resided with his uncle in the Community Garden Trailer Park near the town limits.

He had no children attending Kelby Creek Elementary.

He had no relationship with any of the staff.

He had no reason to do what he had done.

"No one knows every part of a man," Jones said, arms crossed over his chest and watching as another cruiser left. "Everyone in Kelby Creek was given the horrible kindness of learning that after Annie McHale was taken."

Jones let out a sigh that went from spine to belly. An approaching truck from the other end of the parking lot was coming in hot. Carlos tensed for a second.

"I didn't know how long this was going to take so Dad grabbed the neighbor's car to come get Bonnie," he explained before the question was asked.

Jones's father had never been a man to hold back an apology, just as he had never been a man known to give one that he shouldn't. Yet, Jones saw in his father's body language, as soon as he parked and jumped out of the car, that the older man was riddled with misplaced guilt and heading fast to singing sorry.

Jones didn't want to hear it so he met his father between the school's front pavilion and the parking lot, and stopped him before he started.

"There's no way in the world that you could have known what was going to happen today," Jones said, forcing his posture to relax a little. "The only blame that's getting placed is squarely on the shoulders of some man named Bill Burrows."

His father didn't like being talked at about what he should or shouldn't be feeling—a trait Jones had more than inherited—and took to the defensive fast.

"I've known for two whole months that that dang truck of mine needed to get seen about. Had I gone and done it, Bonnie would have already been home with me." He shook his head, in full-on self-loathing mode. A feeling that Jones was also well-versed in.

Jones started to point out, once again, that his father

wasn't to blame, but the door to the school opened farther behind them. They turned to see Bonnie run out, and Jones's father met Bonnie in his own little jog. He crouched down and threw his arms around her in one fluid motion.

Behind her, Jones noted the boy named Keith, his foster mother and Cassandra.

Cassandra West.

Miss Cassandra West.

Miss "Unforgettable and Pregnant" Cassandra West.

Jones let his eyes take her in for a long moment. Her attention was on the conversation with Keith's foster mother, giving him an opening to stare.

She was beautiful, breathtakingly so.

That was true from the moment Jones had seen her to the moment he'd really taken her in while in the library.

Now, though, it was a different look. At the hotel she'd been dressed up, chic. Fashion-forward, at least several steps in front of where Jones was. Her hair had been done neat, and even her eyes, which had captivated him, had a crispness. An edge that he guessed came from experience. What experience that was hadn't mattered then, at the bar, out at dinner, or between the sheets. He wasn't supposed to see her again, after all.

But here she was, wearing a colorful dress with wild, full hair and a streak of glitter across her belly.

Her pregnant belly.

He hadn't had the time to run the numbers between their encounter and today, but when his late wife had been pregnant with Bonnie and showing like Cassandra, she'd been about ready to pop.

Did that mean Cassandra had been pregnant already when they'd met?

Or was Cassandra pregnant because of their meeting?

"Dad! I didn't get in trouble for the fire alarm!"

Bonnie's eager voice broke through his internal questions. He needed to talk to Cassandra, one way or the other, but he wasn't going to jump the line.

Jones put on a smile and joined his father and daughter.

"Nope, you didn't," he said to her. "In this situation pulling the fire alarm was a very good thing, even if there was no fire."

Bonnie beamed as Keith and his mother met them, Cassandra trailing behind. She'd become the unofficial liaison to the group, since no one could get a hold of the principal, vice principal, or superintendent. Coach Rich, the only other person still on the school grounds, was inside talking to one of the firemen who had responded. He seemed more miffed that he'd missed out on the action, rather than that the action had happened at all.

"Is there anything else I need to do before we go?" Keith's foster mom asked. Carlos had been the one to address her earlier.

Carlos gave Jones a quick look. He nodded, but before she could move along, he handed her a business card.

"Millie Lovett contracts with the sheriff's department and helps kids deal with certain stressful situations like today. It's free of charge and DHR-approved in most cases. Just give her a ring."

She didn't look like she was going to make the call, but she took the card all the same.

The little boy started to follow her but Cassandra took his hand. She lowered herself to meet his gaze, careful of her stomach.

"And if you don't end up talking to the nice Mrs. Foster, you can always talk to me," she said to the boy. Jones suspected, though, that her tone was meant for his grown-up. She smiled and tapped the spot over her heart twice. "Pirate's code—I'll always listen."

Jones quirked an eyebrow at that statement, but the boy obviously understood. His voice was a little tearful but he held her gaze when he answered.

"Pirate's code."

His foster mother led him away and Cassandra took a little time standing. She was chewing on a thought and spit it out with a dollop of quiet.

"Mrs. Shaw is a good woman but she's...got a lot on her plate."

Jones, his father and Carlos let that sit. Then it was time to move along. Carlos went back inside to finish up and Jones's father took Bonnie's hand. He promised her a stop to get ice cream, something that made Jones laugh.

"This time don't bother saying you're getting one for me and saving it," he said. "We all know you two just split my cone the second y'all get home."

Bonnie "Miss Sweet Tooth" Murphy put on her most mischievous grin.

It warmed Jones's heart.

Just as much as it almost shattered it.

What had Bill Burrows been up to?

What would have happened had Cassandra not been as fast on her feet?

The woman in question was smiling politely at them. Jones realized, belatedly, he should have introduced them all. At least Cassandra to his father. Apparently, she already knew his daughter.

Instead, he hugged Bonnie and promised his dad he'd be home when he was finished.

Cassandra didn't speak for a moment as they watched them get into the car.

When she did, her voice had taken on yet another pitch. It was soft and this time ever so warm.

"You know, Bonnie did some quick thinking with that fire alarm. Six-year-old me might have kept running."

Jones smiled at that.

"I think some kids thrive under pressure, even when they're scared. Look at that boy, Keith. Bonnie said he refused to leave you and went back to try and help. That's a kid who loves his teacher."

A rose tint went across Cassandra's cheeks.

"It's pirate code. You don't leave your friends behind." She laughed. "Then again, I made that code for our school trip to the aquarium, so he'd be more inclined to want to stay with his field-trip buddy."

Jones wanted to know more about where this pirate code had originated, but what they weren't talking about was too hard to ignore. Cassandra was quickest to the punch.

"So." She motioned to his badge. "This is the job you were considering? Sheriff?"

Jones nodded.

"It was."

"Well, I have to say I'm glad for it." She glanced at the school. It wasn't lost on Jones that he'd been wearing the badge Cassandra had helped him decide to put on while trying to save her.

"This is definitely feeling like a full-circle moment," he responded.

She laughed. There were nerves in it. She ran a hand over her belly. There was no ring on her finger.

Did that mean...?

"So I guess neither one of us did mention that we were from Kelby Creek. That might have changed some things." Cassandra rubbed her belly again. Was it his imagination, or had her eyes gone to his hand, too?

She took a notable deep breath in.

Then notable hesitation.

"Do you think we could talk later?" she added. "Like maybe not at my work or, uh, a crime scene?"

Jones, who had been waiting for her to say something else, nodded.

He took care not to stare down at her pregnant stomach.

"Is tonight too soon? We could grab some food. My place, or maybe Crisp's?"

Jones resisted the urge to make a joke about minibars costing too much, a reference to their first meeting. But that version of him—flying solo in a hotel to think about the future—had been more carefree. A lot more so than the man with the badge standing in front of her now.

He couldn't be that man who had made her laugh at the hotel bar.

Not when he was standing guard over his family and the town. Not when it was Kelby Creek.

"Crisp's sounds great," Cassandra responded quickly. "I can meet you there at seven?"

"Sounds good to me."

She went back to smiling but there was something weighing it down.

Then again, she'd just been through a lot.

Cassandra started to walk away but Jones gently took her elbow. She stopped in her tracks and met his gaze with eyes that seemed to glow. Jones let her go.

"Thank you, again, for what you did today," he said from the bottom of his heart. "You fought to keep the kids safe. You did good. Really good."

Cassandra's voice went back to soft.

"I had no other choice." She shrugged. "Pirate's code."

Jones wanted to say more, wanted to keep talking, but her words coincided with Carlos coming back out of the school and calling to him.

With one last look, Jones and Cassandra parted ways.

"This is the woman? The woman?"

Hours later and Jones's father was handing his son his jacket at his truck and trying, and failing, to keep his curiosity in check.

"Minifridge-joke woman?" his dad added when Jones didn't instantly answer.

He shrugged into his jacket and sighed.

His father was the only person who knew about his time with Cassandra, from their game at the bar to the reason he'd missed his early check-out time. It wasn't that Jones and his father shared every detail about their lives, but not telling someone about Cassandra somehow felt wrong. It might have felt like a dream but he wasn't about to let it be forgotten.

So he'd shared the information. All of it.

Just as he'd keyed his dad into Cassandra's surprise occupation and location in relation to him.

Then he'd had to ask him to babysit Bonnie while Jones went to their more relaxed reunion.

What Jones hadn't expected was his father to get so excited about it all.

"Yes, it's minifridge-joke woman," he finally confirmed, starting his truck so it could warm up. Kelby Creek was only getting colder at night now. "But maybe let's stick with calling her Cassandra."

His dad crossed his arms over his chest and shook his head in disbelief.

"You drove out to that hotel a good four hours away from here and just happened to meet someone who broke through that metal cage around you and now she's teaching Bonnie at Kelby Creek Elementary? If that doesn't make you feel all squiggly inside, I don't know what will."

Jones rolled his eyes. There was a fine line between

answering his dad with a yes or no, and diving into feelings about being squiggly or not. He got into the truck.

"She isn't Bonnie's teacher. She's Bonnie adjacent in a way. She's a kindergarten teacher but not Bonnie's."

His father gave a dismissive snort.

"The same woman you've been pining for all these months was holding your daughter's hand a few hours ago, protecting her. That's something wild and you know it, son."

He did know it but that was neither here nor there right now.

"See you in a few hours," Jones said, slowly shutting his door. "Tell Bonnie I'll come in and check on her when I'm back."

The door closing was a satisfying noise. Seeing his dad now roll his eyes was a bonus.

Kelby Creek at night when it was cold was something else. Something nice. Never a true fan of the cold, Jones nevertheless rolled down the window a little just to feel the cool against his face.

Or, he realized, maybe it was less about feeling the cold as it was trying to calm himself down.

He wouldn't call what he felt squiggly but he wouldn't say that his stomach wasn't a little knotted in nerves.

Nerves that were split, at that.

Jones glanced at the passenger seat and the folder he knew that was under it.

A breakdown of Annie McHale's last day in public was detailed in his own handwriting inside. Notes he'd been taking at his desk when his father had called in about his car trouble. Notes he'd been still thinking about when he'd parked at the elementary school.

The first week that he'd been able to start his investigation into Annie's case and his daughter had been involved in an attack with still no clear motive?

Some chance meetings were a happy coincidence.

This, though?

Jones didn't like this one bit.

Chapter Five

Crisp's Kitchen hadn't changed at all since it had opened when Jones was a kid. Sure, it had changed hands, but the simple decorations and furniture were the same as the printed menus and radio station playing softly from the kitchen.

Yet Crisp's could do a lot of things with the little it had.

The same place where they had their Sunday afternoon family dinners now felt wholly intimate. The lights were warmer, softer, and there were only a few people seated. As Jones walked in he turned his attention to a beautiful woman wearing a long-sleeved dress and smiling.

Jones didn't have to check his watch to know he wasn't late. In fact, he'd planned on coming early and had.

Apparently he hadn't come early enough.

Cassandra didn't get up to greet him, but waved a hand at the seat across from her. She laughed.

"Yes, I got here very early," she said as a greeting. It got a smile out of him. "And, yes, that's one of my things that I do. I arrive early, way earlier than anyone ever should." She raised her hands in mock defense. "It's something I've been working on."

Jones sat down and moved his legs into just the right spot so his knees wouldn't hit the table. This was something he'd practiced after his last growth spurt as a teenager. Being so tall often had small annoyances like that to deal with.

"I can't say anything, I'm up with the sun," he said. "That's more speaking to Bonnie training me quick that babies, toddlers and especially six-year-olds don't believe in sleeping in."

Cassandra's smile straightened out.

"How is Bonnie? Today is going to give me nightmares, can't imagine it on a kiddo."

After finishing up at the school, Jones had let Carlos convince him to go home instead of back to work. He was glad for the push. Part of him wanted to tear apart Bill Burrows's motive and plan, but a bigger part wanted to eat ice cream with his daughter and make sure she was okay.

"We watched her favorite cartoons together and then had a good talk about people doing bad things and emergencies. I'm sure something will crop up about it all, but I'm going to get her in with Millie next week since she has some time in her schedule then. I know you don't teach her directly but I'm thinking you might have noticed that Bonnie is a bit…free-spirited."

He never meant Bonnie's wild streak as an insult, so he made sure to laugh at the last part. It was easy considering Cassandra was already nodding.

"I know at the big Family Picnic party a while back she had to be coaxed down from the big kid jungle gym after climbing to the top and, uh, howling like a wolf."

This time that got Jones. A belly laugh shook him and vibrated into the table.

"That would be on me and my dad. We might have watched a movie where a man turned into a werewolf and climbed on top of a roof and howled to signal his pack." He shrugged. "It was some B-rated horror movie Dad and I were watching and we realized that she was not, in fact, asleep on the couch when it was through."

"Sponges," Cassandra said knowingly. "Children, especially at that age, are dang sponges and soak up anything and everything adults don't want them to."

Jones agreed to that as a waitress came. Deputy Marigold's ex-mother-in-law, Nan. Marigold had made no small show of letting him know that if he wanted a good meal he shouldn't bring up how beloved she was within the department. Marigold had been trying to be funny, of course, but her partner, Sterling, had made sure they all knew it was true. If you wanted a good meal at Crisp's, you didn't mention Marigold's name unless you wanted scowling, grumping and general anger.

"She'll retire one day soon," Marigold had said in the break room when they were talking about lunch spots. "And the day after that happens I'll buy everyone something good."

Today wasn't that day and Nan was in a fine mood. She nodded to Jones.

"Sheriff, been a stretch since you've come in," she

said in greeting. "I was starting to think you didn't like us anymore."

Jones put on his most, he hoped, charming smile.

"It's nothing on this place, Nan. I've just been under piles of work, is all. Best I've been eating is whatever Dad has in the fridge for leftovers, and you know him— he's all about the power of a good sandwich."

Nan, who was in her upper sixties, had known his father since they were both in their thirties.

"It's been a longer stretch since I've seen Ted." She placed her pad on the table, giving up the illusion that she was going to take anything but gossip before she wrote down their order. A look of concern pulled at her brow. "How's he doing, by the way? I heard his knee surgery went okay but there were some issues."

The easiest way to get out of gossip was to simply go through it. Jones kept with the facts.

"Yes, ma'am, the surgery went fine. It was the pain meds that are supposed to help manage the aftermath that we had some issues with. We found out he was allergic and had to stick with the normal over-the-counter meds. He managed fine, though. Still a little stiff at times but he's been off the crutches for months."

Nan nodded and put a hand to her chest as if she had been there through it.

"Bless his heart." Nan surprised him by reaching out to touch his hand. She went full-on staring when she continued. "And bless *your* heart for coming back to take care of that old fool. I know how hard that must've been. Coming back."

Jones wasn't in a pleasant, polite mood anymore. He

felt his smile tighten. He gave one nod. He didn't enjoy being blunt about not wanting to talk about his past.

But he would.

Nan opened her mouth and Jones knew she was about to go right for the jugular.

"I'm so sorry but could I go ahead and order, Nan?" Both Jones and the older woman turned. Cassandra gave her an apologetic smile. "I've just been craving your delicious burger and fries all dang day and I don't think I can go without them much longer. In fact, could I just go ahead and order a cup of sweet tea with that, too? You know how I love your sweet tea."

Nan, clearly miffed at being interrupted, had no choice but to meet the sweet with her own sweet. She slid her writing pad back into her hand.

"Oh, of course, darlin'. I know all about cravings. Let me stop gabbing and get you going. What about you, Sheriff?"

"I'll actually take the same, but a coffee, black, instead of the tea."

Nan nodded, and didn't write anything down.

"I'll get y'all in and be back in a jiffy with your drinks."

Jones and Cassandra thanked her, and then Jones gave another thanks to Cassandra for the save when the older woman was gone. She waved her hand dismissively.

"Nan has a way of digging in on things she has no business digging in on," Cassandra responded. "Her family might make a mean burger, but that's no reason to tell her your whole life story every time you sit down."

Jones leaned back a little. He already felt more relaxed now that Nan was gone. Or, maybe it had to do with his current company. During their night together Jones had felt, for the first time in a long time, lighter.

"You seem to know the routine here pretty good. How long have you lived in Kelby Creek, if you don't mind my asking?"

"Oh, I don't mind." Cassandra waved her hand in another dismissive move. Jones noticed she used her hands to talk a lot, more than most. He wondered now if that had to do with her being a teacher. It was probably easier to get kids to listen when you used your hands to grab their attention.

"I've been here for three years, four in December," she continued. "It's crazy that it's been that long, though sometimes it feels like I've been here forever." She laughed.

Jones didn't.

If she had only been in town for almost four years then she'd missed what had happened. She'd missed the corruption and the town falling apart. She'd missed Annie's kidnapping.

She'd missed him packing up Bonnie and all of their things and driving as fast as he could away from Kelby Creek, not once looking in the rearview.

She'd missed his world crumbling all because of a picnic blanket.

He could have told her that, asked her about what

she knew of The Flood, but instead he was genuinely curious as to why she'd chosen their town.

"I have to say, Kelby Creek isn't usually a destination people strive to visit, let alone move to. Is there a particular reason you picked it? Do you have any kin here?"

Cassandra's smile faltered. It was a brief thing but one that resonated hard in Jones's chest. He was ready to take back his question but she beat him to the answer before he could.

"No, I'm not from here." She was quiet but not so much that she was whispering. "My fiancé lived here for a few years and said it was a good place to start over. When I was looking for my own new start, I saw the job opening at the elementary school and, well, it seemed like a sign."

Jones raised an eyebrow at *fiancé*, even though he hadn't meant it to. Once again he glanced to see her bare ring finger. Was she married now? Engaged? Was she not wearing a ring because she was pregnant?

Helen's fingers had started to swell while she was carrying Bonnie. She'd ditched her wedding band during the second trimester.

Had Cassandra done the same?

Jones was about to rephrase his original question to try and get an answer without outright prodding.

Cassandra, once again, was quick to explain herself without the question.

"He passed away a few weeks before our wedding," she continued. "A car accident. No pain, just didn't make it." Her smile turned watery. Jones knew the feeling all too well.

He reached across the table and placed his hand over one of hers.

"I'm sorry." It wasn't enough—he knew that, too—but he couldn't just say nothing.

Cassandra took her other hand and patted his twice. When she was done, Jones pulled his back. Though the urge to keep it there was tugging at him.

"Thanks," she said. "I just never really know how to refer to him. Some people around here know him as my ex without all of the sad details. Sometimes that's easier than dealing with those who like to take other people's sad stories and spread them for something to talk about."

Jones could have brought up Helen then. Told Cassandra about what had happened at the park that day. Told her about how he'd gone from a new father to a single dad within the space of a few breaths.

Yet, he hesitated.

They both knew loss and he'd never take that from her or discount it because it was different from his, but there was something nasty about the way Helen had gone.

Daggers of salt in a wound torn open so wide you couldn't even see the other side.

Jones froze, wanting to talk about it but unable to muster the energy.

"Not saying the words, doesn't make it any less real, son," his dad had told him during one of his long stays when Bonnie was a baby. "The pain just sits and hollows you out, even when you're not looking."

That was the thing, though.

Jones wasn't keeping quiet about Helen's death because he was in denial. He didn't talk about that horrible day because of one thing and one thing only.

Guilt.

Ravenous, bottomless, dragging, smothering guilt.

That's why Jones couldn't tell Cassandra now about what had happened then.

He didn't want to show that guilt to someone openly showing him their grief.

It wasn't fair to her.

Or her unborn child, cradled inside of her and the only question he'd needed answered since the moment he saw her at the school.

"Speaking of people who seem to enjoy other people's troubles."

Cassandra had put on a smile that Jones now recognized as practiced politeness. He followed her gaze to Nan, who was bustling over to their table with their drinks. The second she put them down she was looking at Jones with noticeable annoyance.

"I know this isn't proper of me but Jimmy is in the back and is asking to talk to you, Sheriff. I told him it's not good manners or business to go after you before you've even had the time to drink a drop, but he's insisting something awful."

Jones shared a look with Cassandra.

"Tell him I have business hours or, at least, that he can wait until I'm done eating with my companion here."

Nan rolled her eyes.

"Wish I could convince him to listen to me for once,

but not a thing in the world I can do to shut him up other than to say I tried. I even told him he could come out here himself but he got all squirrely. Said he doesn't want the rest of the guests here to see him bothering you. Me, though? He has no problem bothering in public."

Under normal circumstances Jones would have told Jimmy "too dang bad," but there was his curiosity keeping the impulse back.

Jimmy was Nan's younger brother and not at all a fan of the Dawn County Sheriff's Department. His dislike, though, hadn't come from The Flood, but was from his younger years as a frequent flyer at the county jail. If he wasn't in cuffs for possession or disorderly, he was behind bars for assault or public intoxication. Sure, he'd found his own redemption after a short stint in prison when he was in his twenties, but now he was a man in his midfifties who was king at holding grudges against any and all law enforcement. The fact that he wanted to talk to someone with a badge was surprising.

The fact that he wanted to talk to the sheriff was downright wild.

Jones shared another look with Cassandra.

She used her hands to talk along with her when she spoke.

"Go on, I promise I don't mind," she said. "I was thinking about checking in with Keith again to make sure he was doing okay."

Jones pushed back his chair.

"You sure?"

Cassandra nodded.

"Go on," she repeated.

Jones didn't like it, but he soon was knocking at the office door at the back of the building. He'd only been inside of the office once when he was a teen. When Jimmy opened the door, however, it was like stepping into a time capsule. Everything was old, dated. Weathered, worn.

Even Jimmy, who was gray and worried.

He didn't beat around the bush after letting in Jones.

"You grabbed Bill from the school today, but did he have anything with him?"

Jones knew that the story of what happened at the school had already been teased on the social-media account of the local news, but none of the names had been released. Still, Jones wasn't surprised the details had traveled fast.

"You know I can't talk about ongoing investigations, Jimmy. Those are the rules."

Jimmy shook his head. Jones saw urgency and aggression in the movement.

"I don't care about no rules, I just want to know if you found his bomb or not."

That was a surprise.

"What do you mean, his bomb?"

Jimmy was as expressive as Cassandra, but with a whole heap of worry added in.

"The other night at the bar he got to talking and said he knew how to make a bomb from his time in the military and could use it to get this town out of the past and into something new if he really wanted to. We thought he was just talking to talk—he's like that, you know?—

but then I heard about him attacking kids at the school and, well, I got that bad feeling. The one in your gut that tells you to get going."

Jones already had his phone out.

"If it was him today, and I'm not saying it was, there was nothing recovered on him or his car. Same with his house." Carlos had led those searches, along with Detective Lovett.

But that wasn't sitting right with Jimmy. He shook his head again.

"If he ever made anything it would have been with Miles, his ex's son," he said. "Miles idolizes him and is old enough to drive. He'd do whatever that man asked him to do and I can't seem to find him anywhere. That's what scares me, Sheriff. If Bill wasn't just talking and y'all didn't find anything, then what if that boy got talked into something worse than attacking kids on the playground?"

The last headshake was one of complete anxiety.

Jones felt it transfer through the man's final words.

"All I know is, if I was you, Jones, I'd want to find that boy before he found you and yours."

Chapter Six

Lila Shaw, Keith's foster mother, said that Keith had been fine all night until when it was time to get ready for bed.

"He's in his room, quiet as a mouse, but won't lie down. I'm about to try and talk to him. Maybe read something to distract him," Lila said on the phone. Cassandra told her that she thought that was a good idea.

"Maybe stay away from pirate books, if you can. We talked a lot about the pirate code earlier and it might trigger him."

Lila seemed confused by the directive, but agreed to read the book her former foster child had left with her about space travel.

Keith would like that and hopefully get some sleep, Cassandra thought. If not, she'd be loving on him extra the next day just in case.

The conversation ended there. It had been quick.

But not as quick as Jones, and the man who must have been Jimmy, who came out of the back and hurried toward the table.

"I'm so sorry, Cassandra," Jones said, cell phone in

his hand. "But I have something urgent that I need to see to. Can I call you later?"

He was stressed. Tenfold. It could be seen in the crease above his brow, the flare of his nostrils and how his posture had gone from casual and relaxed to stiff.

Something was happening.

And it put anxiety into her veins.

"Yeah, sure," she said. "Go ahead."

Jones didn't prod her again to make sure she was okay with it. One second he was there, the next he and Jimmy were bustling out.

It happened so quickly that Cassandra didn't realize she'd never given her phone number to Jones until he was already gone.

Disappointment mixed with and an exhaustion that had become familiar since she'd seen those two red lines on her pregnancy test.

Nan appeared at her side, flustered.

"Your food's ready. Jimmy said it's on the house. Do you still want it?"

Her earlier sweetness had dried up. Nan was confused and worried, too. That didn't mean Cassandra wanted to stay.

"Could I have it in a to-go box, please?" she asked. "My back is starting to ache and I wouldn't mind stretching out."

Nan nodded absently and was back before Cassandra could collect herself.

"Have a good one," she told the older lady.

Nan smiled, then pulled out her cell phone. She was

staring at it when Cassandra was walking to the front doors.

Kelby Creek was cold tonight.

Cassandra breathed in air that cooled her lungs and calmed her soul. She had a jacket in her car, but had been too hot to wear it earlier. Too nervous at seeing Jones and telling him some news that was going to rock his world.

A world that, apparently, was already rocking.

Nan being passive-aggressive as she'd tried to pry into his homecoming hadn't been missed by Cassandra. Neither were Jones's several looks at her pregnant stomach.

He wanted to ask who the father was, as much as she was worried about telling him it was him.

Cassandra still didn't know if Jones was married, if he was seeing someone, if his interest in being a father only extended to Bonnie.

Though, whatever his situation was, it didn't change Cassandra's.

She was going to be a mom to a little boy she hadn't yet thought of a name for and she was as nervous as she was excited to meet him.

How Jones wanted to factor into that didn't change her feelings on her son.

But what if Jones does want to be a family? What if he wants your son all to himself? Joint custody? Marriage and a house with a white picket fence? What if he wants nothing to do with us at all?

These were questions Cassandra hadn't had to answer before since she hadn't known where in the world Jones might be.

Now?

Now she could see him in the car-pool pickup line, or at the grocery store, or in line at the bank.

Their time together at the hotel had felt like a dream.

Now the consequences of that night were about to bring them to a new reality.

And it terrified Cassandra because she had no idea what she hoped Jones wanted.

"At least now we have another night to stress over it," she told her pregnant belly once she was behind the wheel of her car. "I hope you're ready for burgers, fries and ice cream, baby boy. Because that's on the menu as soon as we get home."

Cassandra pulled out of the parking lot and was surprised to pass Jimmy standing next to a car, talking expressively on his phone. She had thought he was going someplace with Jones, but maybe he couldn't because he wasn't the law. That got Cassandra wondering about what could have been that urgent as she made her way toward Wayne's Road.

She lived in the neighborhood of Holly Oak and the quickest way across town without going through a ton of lights and four-way stops was Wayne's Road. It was relatively scenic but had enough lighting that taking it at night didn't feel like a total gamble on safety.

And then there was Cassandra's thing about driving.

If she could avoid as many drivers as possible, she tried.

Cassandra passed by a stretch of woods on one

side, an open field on the other. The stars were in full
bloom and the spaces between the streetlights were wide
enough to see them.

It was nice for a bit, all things considered.

Even when she saw the taillights, she was glad to
only see the one set.

Though, they were disappearing fast in the distance.

Too fast.

Cassandra slowed down. Something wasn't quite
right. There was fog around the edge of the bridge up
ahead. She peered through the windshield, squinting
since the nearest lights were yards behind her.

The bridge was old, with guardrails made of metal
and wood. While the creek that wound its way through
town was narrow in parts, this spot let the waterway
breathe and stretch, was not so much wide as deep.

Cassandra slowed the closer she got.

Then she pulled onto the grass shoulder, right above
the slope down to the creek bed.

Part of the guardrail was gone and the fog was definitely not fog.

It was smoke.

Cassandra flung open her door and ran onto the
bridge. The smoke was coming out of the truck that
was currently sinking down into the water below.

A truck whose doors and windows were shut.

Whoever was driving was still inside.

"Hold on!"

Cassandra didn't know if her voice carried below or
not, since the drop was at least ten feet down, but she
didn't stand still to check.

She'd prepared for this.

She knew what to do.

Cassandra ran back to her car and opened the center console. She grabbed what she needed, put it in her pocket and swiped her phone as she maneuvered down the sloped grass. Her call to 911 was fast and efficient.

She knew more than most that time mattered in these situations. Seconds were precious.

She wasn't going to waste hers.

"A truck ran off of the bridge on Wayne's Road. It's going underwater," she yelled as soon as the dispatcher answered. "I think someone is still inside."

The grass was slick, or maybe she had more adrenaline in her than she realized.

Either way, Cassandra made it to the water's edge and pulled out her pocket-size flashlight, her legs shaking.

Dispatch started talking but Cassandra was focused on her beam of light as it skated across the front of the truck being covered by the water. When the beam landed on the driver, she found her words quickly.

"Oh, my God, it's Jones," she yelled into the phone. "It's Sheriff Murphy!"

PAIN.

In his head and along his right leg.

Jones reasoned it probably hurt more at the moment of the collision than it did when he'd regained consciousness, but seeing as he'd also been knocked clean out, there was no way to tell.

He just groaned as he rejoined the land of the living

and had a hard time placing where he was and why he was there in the first place.

There had been the school, then ice cream with Bonnie, then Cassandra...

Then Billy.

Which had led to Jones getting all the information he could about Miles before peeling out of the parking lot in the direction of his house.

But why was Jones...?

The truck around him shuddered. He realized belatedly that he wasn't on the road anymore. He was tilted, downward. But he was moving.

Jones heard a splash. Then he felt the familiar sway that he'd only ever experienced on a boat.

Finally, the rest of the details surrounding his new reality pieced together.

He'd been run off of the Wayne's Road Bridge. Meaning he was now in a truck that was in creek water deep enough to drown him, if he didn't get going.

Jones went to his seat belt as water slapped against his window. In his time as deputy, he'd seen a car go off into water not as deep as the spot he was in. The only reason the man had been able to get out when he did was because his door had already been open before water pressure had sealed it shut. Jones had had no idea he was about to go for a swim, or else he would have done the same. Now he tried to open the door and it didn't do a thing. He went to the power window next. The lights went out as the engine drowned. The button under his finger did nothing.

Jones unbuckled his seat belt and reached over for

his cell phone. It wasn't there and he didn't have time to find it. He was going to have to break his window or else risk not being able to escape when the vehicle went to the bottom of the creek.

He went for his gun next, deciding to go ahead and use that to get out. Yet, as was his luck tonight, he remembered it was stashed in his holder in the glove compartment. The locked glove compartment.

Jones fumbled for his keys but knew he'd lost his opening to do what he needed to do.

The water was rising.

Bonnie came to the front of his mind like a slap to the face. Then his father.

Then—

"Jones!" He thought he'd imagined it or manifested it somehow. A muffled voice, there at his window. He turned to see that voice wasn't just a figment of his imagination, but was coming from a woman treading water next to his door.

Not just any woman.

Cassandra put one hand on the truck to keep her steady. She had something in her other hand. It was orange and small, but she reared her arm back, ready to use it.

"Cover your eyes!"

Jones didn't have time to ask why. He shielded his eyes just as a *tink* sounded against the window. That *tink* sounded one more time before something new gave way.

Glass.

Breaking.

Cassandra had one of those car-escape tools. Ones meant to break windows in an emergency.

Jones could have kissed her when he felt some glass land on his lap.

He might have done it if water hadn't come in, too.

"Hurry!" Cassandra was yelling but had done the main job. Now she used her little orange hammer to clear away the rest of the glass.

Jones undid his belt and started to make his way out of the window, when the water finally got its fingers all the way around the car.

Instead of slowly sinking, he went from seeing Cassandra and the night sky to being underwater.

He was pushed against his seat and soaked.

But he wasn't trapped anymore.

Cassandra had seen to that.

SHE HAD NEVER been the greatest of swimmers and she wasn't sure how long she could safely hold her breath while pregnant, but Cassandra plugged her nose and knew she had to try.

She took a deep breath and felt her muscles move as she readied to dive when something touched her arm.

The yell that escaped her was partially filled with water.

It didn't stop Cassandra from saying his name when Jones broke the surface right next to her.

"Are you okay?" she asked, bobbing up and down.

Jones answered by putting his arm around her waist. He pulled her along with him as he swam them a few feet over to the shallow part of the creek. Despite finding their footing, he kept her close to him until they were out of the water. He let her go and touched his head, wincing.

There was blood.

Cassandra's worry started to climb again, but Jones was all eyes on her.

"Are *you* okay?"

Cassandra was.

She knew she was.

All she'd done was swim a little, use her emergency tool a little more and then tread water.

She was *fine* physically.

But, man, her emotions were rough.

The blood on his head, his completely soaked clothes, the image of him not moving in the driver's seat...?

What if Cassandra hadn't been there?

Would he have made it out?

Or would he have died, at the bottom of the creek, never knowing...?

It was all too much and Cassandra did the only thing that she could think of in the moment.

"He's yours," she blurted out. Her hands went to her stomach. "The baby. He's yours."

The sound of a siren whirled in the distance.

Jones's eyes stayed right on her.

Chapter Seven

"I—I was going to tell you earlier, but I was trying to wait for the right moment." Cassandra motioned generally around them. "I know this wasn't it, but I—I had to make sure you knew."

Jones, bless him, didn't ask if she was sure. Though, he did have one question.

"Did you say a boy?"

Cassandra's heart melted a little.

"Yes. A boy."

Jones took a step forward, face still impassive. The sirens had become louder. He stopped and looked to the road.

"Is your car up there?"

Cassandra's heart fell a little at that, even though she knew it wasn't the time to talk about their baby or their future.

"Yeah. Flashers on, too. And my phone is, uh, somewhere over there and should still be on with Dispatch." Cassandra pointed to the spot she'd dropped her phone after seeing Jones with his eyes closed. She figured she'd already told them all of the pertinent information they needed to know. Sheriff unconscious in a sinking truck next to Wayne's Road Bridge.

"Come on." Jones took her hand and led her to her dropped phone before taking them both back up the slope of grass that led to the road. He was cold, she realized, as she was shivering. They both must have looked like something wild when a cruiser pulled up behind her car.

A man she didn't recognize jumped out of the driver's seat, while a man she did, Sterling Costner, tore out of the passenger side. His signature cowboy hat was missing and he was actively stripping out of his coat when his eyes landed on them.

"Sheriff!" It was two syllables but it did a fine job of conveying absolute relief and confusion. "What's going on?"

Cassandra hadn't had time to wonder how Jones had made it into the creek, just that he had been there, but now she tilted up a curious chin to his answer.

"I was burning rubber to Miles's house when a car came out of nowhere. Slammed into my side. Hit my head somewhere between that and the water."

The other deputy ran to the bridge and looked over its edge.

"The truck's gone," Jones added. "Only reason I'm above water is because Miss West here thinks quicker than most people blink." He glanced back at the cruiser. "You got a blanket in there?"

Sterling nodded and rushed off, returning in a few seconds with a heavy coverlet that Jones draped over her shoulders. She accepted it with a quick thanks.

"I got a bead on the car. A silver or beige Taurus. I couldn't tell with the lighting. Front left headlight was out."

"I saw a car speeding off that way when I came up and saw the bridge." Cassandra pointed ahead of them.

The other deputy backtracked. More sirens sounded in the distance.

"Want in, or want to stay?" The question was to Jones. Of course it was—he was the sheriff. Still, Cassandra felt a ping of panic at the choice. First of all, Jones was hurt. Blood was clearly at his hairline and he'd already admitted to losing consciousness.

Not to mention, both of them were soaked in the cold.

"Go ahead. I'm staying here."

Jones's words were heavy and final.

Sterling didn't follow up. He was back to the cruiser in a flash.

"EMT is en route. Marigold should be pulling up right before them," he called over the hood of the car. "Foster is on Miles."

Jones nodded and together they watched the car speed off.

"Do you think it was an accident?" Cassandra shivered as she said the words. Jones took her hand again and walked her to her car. He opened the door and cranked the engine. She didn't understand why until he reached inside and fiddled with the air-conditioner controls. More aptly, the heat. Cassandra heard it click on.

Jones stood straight again. He'd been thinking of his answer.

"No," he said simply.

"But why? Why would someone do that? Because you're sheriff?"

At this, he stood in front of her and looped one hand inside of her coat under the blanket. She could feel the weight of him against her. It was comforting and distracting all at once.

"I've been sheriff for months now," he began. Cassandra realized he was trying to take off her coat. She let him, easing out of it as he stepped around her. "But today my daughter has been chased by a man who had no reason to chase her and I've been run off of the road only hours later."

Cassandra had completely forgotten about what had happened at school while she'd been dealing with the sinking truck. Now her acute worry at seeing him get close to drowning evened out into a blanket of anxiety that weighed her down.

"You think it's connected?" she asked.

Jones threw her jacket on top of the car and then took her hand again.

"All you all right?" he asked. "You shouldn't have been in that cold water. Neither one of you."

"I'm fine," she responded. "We're both fine."

He moved her gently to the passenger's seat. Cassandra silently took the directive and lowered herself into the warm interior. Heated air hit her face and stomach directly just as the sirens in the distance became flashing lights seen clearly in the rearview.

Jones glanced back at them but answered her before dealing with the newcomers.

"I might think that it was all some kind of coincidence had this morning been normal routine for me."

Cassandra gave him a questioning look.

"What happened this morning?"

Eyes as deep and serious as the creek they'd just struggled to get free of met Cassandra's and held them fast.

"I found out someone was lying in the Annie McHale investigation."

A LOT OF information came in all at once. Jones met the first wave in the hallway of the sheriff's department.

"Miles is in Oklahoma with his mother," Detective Foster Lovett said, voice low. "He's also ten and hasn't been to Kelby Creek since his mother and Bill ended things when he was four."

Jones crossed his arms over his chest. His shirt didn't like the movement too much. It was tight and a loaner from Sterling, the only Kelby Creek officer who came close to his size. Thankfully, Jones had his workout joggers and tennis shoes in his office so he didn't have to scrounge for pants or footwear. It felt odd to wear the mismatched outfit with his badge. He was, at least, glad he had the shining star. It was the only piece of his uniform he'd had on him as the water had overtaken the truck.

"So he's probably not out here building bombs and singing Bill Burrows's praises," he said, deadpan.

"Not unless he can magically transport himself across the country without his mom, his Boy Scout troop and his little brother catching on, no. I'm going to assume not."

"Then that means Jimmy was either very ill-informed or he told one heck of a lie."

Foster nodded.

"I figured you'd want to ask him yourself about that."

Foster eyed the sheriff's office behind Jones. His wife, Millie, and Cassandra were inside. Both women had been told they could go home and both women had wanted to stay for answers. Though, Jones had a sneaking suspicion that Cassandra was still worried about him. When the EMT had checked out the cut on his head, she'd been hovering nearby, insisting he go to the emergency room. The last he had heard they were in deep conversation about Millie's job as a social worker for the county.

When Foster made another quick glance that way, Jones decided to give the man a bone. His wife had already brought something for Cassandra to change into and he himself had left family dinner to scour the town for Miles and Bill's possible bomb.

"What's on your mind, Lovett?"

Foster put on a smile that was partially apologetic. His voice went even lower than it had before.

"I just didn't know you were dating, is all."

Jones had known Foster before The Flood and had been happy to see him as the lead detective when Jones had become sheriff. He trusted him. Jones knew that he was a good man. He also knew he was a better detective.

Jones wasn't about to waste both of their time by trying to fib out an excuse.

"We weren't on a date, just trying to catch up," he answered. "We had a few moments a while back before parting ways. We didn't even know each other lived in Kelby Creek until what happened at the school today."

That was a very vague way to say something big because their "few moments" had, apparently, become a child.

A baby boy.

Jones had already suspected, based on the timing alone, but hearing Cassandra tell him that he was the father had been a sucker punch.

To the stomach?

The heart?

Both?

He didn't know.

The only feeling he could grasp was that guilt, and it ran deep and spanned years. He'd had to deal with it when Helen was pregnant with Bonnie, and when he'd picked out pink paint for the nursery and hummed some song he never figured out the name of.

Happy, healthy, unable to hold in her excitement at the vision of watching their child grow and be happy and healthy and have their own excitement.

But that wasn't how Helen's story ended.

All because of The Flood, all because of Annie McHale's kidnapping, all because Jones hadn't seen the bad right in front of him.

So when Cassandra was there, risking herself to save *him* while carrying their son?

Jones had done the only thing he knew to be right in that moment.

He'd taken a cold woman to find some warmth and become the sheriff at the scene.

That's what he needed to be now, too.

The sheriff of the department.

Foster, knowing he wasn't going to get more than that answer, nodded. He had the great good sense to set aside his curiosity and cleared his throat. He thumbed back down the hall toward the interrogation room.

"Well, I suggest you get going on Jimmy before he spooks and lawyers up. I don't think he realizes that we've found Miles and also not any kind of bomb, never mind in connection with Bill."

Foster didn't have to tell him twice.

The Dawn County Sheriff's Department had two interrogation rooms. Both were always thoroughly cleaned after use, but one always had a slight dingy feeling to it. Fluctuating temperature, a chair that wobbled just a little and a smell that ran between a hint of mold mixed with staleness all created an uncomfortable feeling for those sitting inside.

That was the room they had Jimmy sitting in. The door was open and maybe that gave him the idea to look a little cocky. But, bad day for him, Jones shut the door tight when he walked in.

"Hey there, Jimmy."

Jones took the chair that didn't wobble and dropped down into it with a sigh. Jimmy's eyes widened a bit but Jones wasn't sure if that was because of his current outfit, or if it was because he wasn't currently on the bottom of the creek. Jones decided to address both in the moment.

"I hope you don't mind my clothes. I know they're not up to snuff for the sheriff, but, well, the damnedest thing happened after I left you in the parking lot earlier." Jones leaned forward, placing his elbows on the table between them. "A car actually ran me off the road, just like in the movies. I went off of a bridge, even. Straight into the water until it ate up my dad's old truck." Jones swooped his hand through the air to pantomime the car going over the edge of the bridge. Jimmy watched the movement. "Thank goodness for one of those emergency hammer things, or else I might not be sitting here across from you right now."

Jones clasped his hands together. He dropped his fake politeness as fast as his truck had dropped into the water.

"But, look at that, I am here now. Sitting with you."

Jimmy, a man who never minded talking, was awfully quiet. If he hadn't had a clue what the mood was, now Jones suspected he was catching on.

"That's rough." That was all he managed to say after it was clear Jones wasn't going to keep on talking. "Some people really need to go back to school to learn about driving. All ages, not just the young'uns."

Jones didn't respond. He didn't nod, and he didn't move an inch. He kept his gaze planted on the smaller man.

The silent treatment was effective when Bonnie used it on Jones; he'd learned that effectiveness still rang true when used in questioning.

People weren't innately fans of the quiet.

That was true for Jimmy after a few more moments

of it. He readjusted his posture, jumped a little when the chair wobbled at the movement and went to talking quick.

"I was going to follow you, like I...like I said, you know, earlier but then I got this call in the parking lot and had to take it," he began. "My nephew, you know the one that was married to Mari—Marigold, I mean—well, he called all upset about some date he was on not going the way he wanted. I couldn't leave him all upset like that, you know, so I was trying to figure out what was what. That's—that's why I didn't follow you or else I woulda seen whoever did that and, well, you know, help you."

Jones unlaced his fingers and rubbed at his chin.

"Your nephew was on a bad date and upset about it," Jones repeated.

Jimmy nodded. He was starting to sweat.

"Must've been really bad considering we were on the way to try and find a teenager with a bomb. One who, according to you, was going to use it to hurt me and mine."

Jimmy went still.

So still it was almost impressive. Like he was a robot who'd just been turned off. Jones marveled at it a moment before Jimmy appeared to restart.

His movements this time were more rigid.

"I love my family," he said. "Nothing more important."

Jimmy was no longer babbling. His tone had gone flat.

Jones didn't understand why. So he took a leap to find out.

"It probably helped matters that you knew Miles wasn't in town—hasn't been in town for years—and held no soft spot for Bill. That's not even mentioning that he's only ten. Also probably helped your conscience to know that there was never any mention of a bomb by Bill."

Jimmy's eyes widened. He didn't confirm, he didn't deny. Which, in itself, was loud.

Jones leaned forward again but not into a casual position. He was getting mad.

"See, the thing is, Jimmy, I'm pretty sure you told me that wild story to get me moving. To get me out on the road. And I think you knew that I'd take Wayne's Road so I could speed my tail off because, well, a bomb's a pretty damn urgent situation. Then, I'm guessing, you found a reason to stay back because, even though you needed to get me out and going, you didn't need to be the person who was supposed to meet me out on the road. But, what I don't get, is the why of it all. Is it because of me arresting Bill?"

Jones had lived through many a surprise in his career in law enforcement. Runners, fighters, people who had nothing in their hands one moment and then holding a weapon the next. He'd used those experiences and his career to become better at spotting the subtle changes, the barely hidden emotions. The spark that was about to ignite a fire that he didn't need to get burned by.

Yet, for all of his experiences, Jones never suspected what the man said next.

Jimmy, a man who'd had a clean record for upward

of twenty years with no real issues, sat to his full height. His words were ice.

"You're going to destroy this town and we're not going to let that happen."

Jimmy leaped across the table.

It was only when Jones reacted and pushed back that he saw the knife in the man's hand.

Chapter Eight

Everyone was running, most were yelling.

Cassandra was standing behind Millie while her husband told her to lock the door behind him. She listened but with extreme hesitance.

Cassandra had her hand on her stomach when the yelling stopped. Millie shared a look with her, but neither one of them spoke until a few minutes passed and Millie's phone vibrated. It was a text.

"Foster said everything's okay," she informed Cassandra as she read. "He said to give them a minute and he'll be back."

The words were reassuring, but the locked door between them and the rest of the department was not. Cassandra was tired of all of the adrenaline that had been pumped into her system that day, and all of the worry, too.

However, the day she was having didn't seem to compare to the day that Jones was.

It was part of the reason she had insisted on coming back to the department with him in the first place. He had been through the stress of a parent seeing his child in jeopardy and a head trauma within hours of each other. The man should have been at home.

Then again, she probably should have been, too.

Cassandra was looking at the clock over Jones's desk when footsteps echoed outside of the door. It was ten o'clock at night and Chief Deputy Park told Millie it was finally okay to come out.

"Where's Foster?" she immediately asked, voice pitching up into a higher octave. Park put his hands up in quick defense.

"He's fine," he said. "He's dealing with a suspect right now and wanted to make sure he got in a few questions before he was sent to the hospital. The suspect, not Foster."

Park shifted his gaze to Cassandra.

"The sheriff asked me to escort you home, if that's all right. He would do it himself but he's…busy right now."

The man probably hadn't meant to, but the way he said the word *busy* came out all wrong.

Cassandra knew she had no real claim to Jones—she wasn't his girlfriend or his wife, just a onetime lover recently reunited—and the fact that she was pregnant with his child really didn't change anything about that. Yet, she gave Park a look she reserved for stubborn kindergartners.

"You tell him I'm fine waiting until I can talk to him myself."

Just like Park had said *busy* all wrong, Cassandra knew how she'd spoken had resonated as something that the man was better off not fighting.

He nodded.

"You did save his life earlier, so he at least owes you a good-night."

Park led both women down one hall, across a large room and down another hall. The first two spaces were devoid of people, but the room they entered was filled with chattering men and women in uniform.

Their sheriff stood off to the side, shirtless and bleeding.

"Oh, my God."

The sudden appearance of Cassandra and Millie barely registered with anyone inside of the room. Whatever happened was way more interesting than a pregnant elementary-school teacher suddenly in their break room.

Jones, however, looked up in an instant.

Then he rolled his eyes at Park.

"You had one job," he said. "One stinking job."

Cassandra ignored both men and moved to Jones. She stopped right in front of him, eyes going straight to the cut on his side.

"What happened?" she asked. "This isn't from the crash, is it?"

Jones sighed, the sound heavy and true.

"No. This is from a conversation that took an unexpected turn."

Cassandra knew that Jimmy had been brought in to get more answers about his accusations about some teenager and a bomb, but she didn't understand how that had gone to Jones being shirtless and bloody less than five minutes after she'd seen him.

"Wait. Jimmy did this?"

This time the sheriff wasn't as forthcoming with his answer. Instead, he grabbed for the first-aid kit open next to him on the counter. It gave him time to construct a vague statement.

"There's a lot of questions still up in the air right now. Don't worry, though, I'm also itching for answers."

Cassandra watched as he took a sanitation wipe and moved it across the cut. The wound didn't look deep and the man didn't wince at the pressure.

"Let Park escort you home," he added. "He's a good man and I trust him. He also said he didn't mind."

A deputy close to them glanced over at Cassandra. It prompted her to take a small step forward. She lowered her voice so only Jones could hear.

"I think you should be the one to go home," she said. "I mean, haven't you been through enough today? Surely somebody else can do a little work while you take at least a little rest?"

Jones gave her a calculating look.

It caught her off guard.

So did his demeanor as it shifted to something more stony.

"I have to go over some things here before I can go home," he said. "And that's probably going to take a while. I can get rest later. *You* should probably think about getting rest now."

He eyed her stomach with quick purpose.

And it put straight anger into her veins.

"Just because I'm pregnant doesn't mean I'm glass," she countered. "And if I can't get you to take a much-needed break, then you don't have any say so about when I should and shouldn't rest, either."

Cassandra understood enough about trauma, herself and pregnancy to know that her anger was coming from a lot of places.

First of all, he was right. She did need to rest. Plain and simple. She was pregnant and she'd been through two significant situations that had been terrifying in their own right.

Secondly, she knew that not getting that rest had made her truly exhausted and, even before pregnancy, a tired Cassandra was never a good Cassandra to be reasonable with.

Lastly, there was a good chance that she was still afraid that something was going to happen to the father of her child. And that held weight. Weight that had her a little panicked.

Plus, there was also the bonus detail that being pregnant often meant being a little hormonal. The week before, she'd all-out sobbed at a grocery-store commercial about buying the right kind of bread from the bakery. It only made sense that seeing Jones again after all of these months on top of seeing Jones hurt was stirring up a lot of those more pronounced reactions.

Still, just because she knew why she was feeling the way she was, didn't stop the feelings from happening.

Before Jones could try and convince her to go, Cassandra decided to listen to him. But, of course, she wanted to make it feel like it was her decision.

She spun around on her heel, hoped that she wasn't making a scene and found Deputy Park next to the door.

"I don't need you to escort me to my house, but if you're offering to walk me to my car, I'll take it."

JIMMY WASN'T TALKING to anyone the next day and no one knew exactly why. His warning, attack and lie about a bomb made no sense. Not to his friends, his coworkers and certainly not to his sister, Nan.

Most concerning was Bill Burrows's lack of connection with Jimmy. As far as any of them could tell they weren't even friends.

"I have never seen Bill around Jimmy," Nan had said, sounding like someone who prided herself on knowing everything and yet was surprised by something unknown so close to home. Jones had questioned her late last night, and she hadn't been happy to be called to the station. "I can count on my hand how many times Bill's been to the restaurant and of those times he hasn't been sitting there talking to Jimmy about nothing. Don't you go saying those two are the same kind of man. Bill went after kids, Jimmy went after the law. And, if you don't remember, that was something the whole town did pretty hard a few years back."

She hadn't wanted to talk to Jones after that. She wanted a lawyer for her brother, though Jimmy had done one smart thing and had already called one in.

"It truly could not be connected," Carlos offered as the end of the shift came near, the long previous night and new day now over.

But Jones wasn't so sure.

"It's the 'we' part of what Jimmy said that has me thinking that something else is going on," Jones said.

"And even if the two incidents aren't connected there are still two different problems." Jones held up his index finger before holding up his middle. He ticked off each as he made his points. "What was Bill trying to do at the school and why did Jimmy come after me?"

"Don't forget about who was the one who tried to get you after Jimmy sent you off on that wild-goose chase about the bomb?"

"There is that."

No questions got answered by the time Carlos convinced him to leave.

"You went home for an hour and then you came back here raring to go," he said. "Miss West was right. You need rest. The department can handle it from here."

Jones was surprised he didn't bring up their friend, and the former sheriff, Brutus Chamblin. During his last stint as interim sheriff, he'd suffered a heart attack on the job. It was during a singularly intense event, but the stress and long hours he'd been swimming in had put him on the road to it. Sure, he had a few years on Jones, but that didn't mean Jones was going to go nose-to-the-gravel, not stopping until he saw blood. He spotted the picture of Bonnie on his desk instead and sighed deeply.

"Call my cell if anything happens."

Carlos seemed surprised, though he didn't say anything out loud.

"Isn't it at the bottom of the creek?" he asked. "Don't tell me that waterproof phones these days are *that* good."

"Definitely not," Jones said. "No amount of rice

could save it. Dad gave me one of his old ones. I had all of my numbers transferred at lunch."

Carlos whistled low. Then sobered.

"I still can't believe that happened. Every year I hope to say this job has been boring, but every year here I am shaking my head and wondering if it's something in the drinking water."

Carlos wasn't alone in wishing for a boring year.

What Jones didn't tell his chief deputy was that he'd already known things were going to get interesting before they settled.

And that had everything to do with the folder that had been destroyed by the water while riding shotgun beneath the passenger seat in Jones's truck.

It felt like a lifetime ago but had only been yesterday morning, when Jones had met someone to talk about the Annie McHale kidnapping.

Then *it* had happened.

I found out someone was lying in the Annie McHale investigation.

Jones shouldn't have told Cassandra that, but it was as true as the need for answers.

He'd caught someone in a lie and, as far as he could tell, it was the first time the lie had been said.

Jones hadn't had the time to process it yet given his father's call to get him to the elementary school and the downward spiral after that.

And maybe that was the point?

Jones growled into the cab of his rental after leaving the department when his talk with Carlos was through.

This was what Kelby Creek had felt like after The

Flood. All the uncertainty, the questions. How everything felt like it was coming at you from every direction.

It was infuriating.

It was frustrating.

It…

Jones cut off his own mental downward spiral. The
sign for Holly Oaks went past his window. His father's.
house wasn't in Holly Oaks.

But he realized he knew someone's house that was.

Jones went to the second street and the third house
on the left. A car was parked in the drive. He parked
behind it and took a moment to look the two-story up
and down.

It was nice. The landscaping, too. There was a wreath
on the front door that looked like only succulents. A
Home Sweet Home sign stood propped up against one
wall of the front porch. Jones spotted the Welcome
doormat. He could see the rainbow printed beneath
the word.

Jones took a deep breath and followed it out into
the cold.

He kept steady and true as he walked up the drive
and across the sidewalk, and when he pressed the doorbell.

He was resolute in his decision to come here, unan-
nounced, and at dusk.

He was sure as sure could be that it needed to be
done.

He needed to be *here*.

Yet, the moment the door opened, the man once

called "the towering sheriff" by a reporter felt two inches tall.

Cassandra might have been wearing an outfit that reminded Jones of a Christmas tree covered in glitter, but her face held nothing but anger.

"I should have called," he said quickly. "And a lot earlier than now, but—"

Cassandra shook her head as she cut him off.

"I know why Bill came after us yesterday." There was no waver or uncertainty in her voice. "And I need you to take me somewhere to prove it."

Chapter Nine

It was five in the afternoon and Cassandra grabbed her third bag of fruit snacks since coming home from school. Or, actually, Jones did, after she waved him into her home.

"So you think that Lila Shaw, Keith's foster mom, was having an affair with Bill," he mused after her hurried follow-up. She didn't ask, but Jones grabbed another bag of fruit snacks from the back of the pantry and moved it down to a lower shelf as he spoke.

Cassandra nodded emphatically.

"Keith ended up taking lunch with just me in the classroom so he could have some space to talk. I could tell something had him quiet, but I just assumed it was what happened. But *then* he said that he didn't know why Bill chased us since the last time he saw him he was so nice."

Cassandra was doing her version of a grid search of the first floor, looking for her purse. Pregnancy brain was certainly real for her, especially when it came to misplacing her things. The week before she'd had to get June to pick her up because she couldn't for the life of her find her keys.

They'd been in the fridge next to a box of cereal. The milk had been in the pantry.

Cassandra had already looked in both places for her bag. Jones dutifully followed her around.

"After that comment I asked a few strategic questions, and according to Keith, who, by the way, I trust, Bill frequented their house…but only when Lila's husband, Joel, was away."

"Bill and Lila were having an affair," Jones said, finishing her theory.

"That's what I'm thinking." They'd made it to the laundry room. Her purse was on top of the dryer, along with a jacket half covered in glitter. The casualty of the day.

"What if Bill thought Keith was about to spill the beans to Joel? What if Keith already had and Bill was coming for, I don't know, revenge?"

"What if Keith isn't the reason at all why Bill was there?"

Cassandra slung her purse across her shoulder. It put the bag on her belly. She readjusted as she gave the sheriff an incredulous look.

"I checked Joel's social media. He checked his marital status to 'separated' *three* days ago. Then *yesterday* his wife's lover chases down his kid? And after Lila told us yesterday that she didn't know Bill that well?"

Jones considered that for a moment. She could tell the line of thought intrigued him.

"Okay, say you're right," he said, changing his stance to arms over his chest. It made an already intimidating man seem all the more giantlike. "What exactly is your plan now?"

Cassandra had seen the man naked, *felt* him naked; there was no reason to be shy about a possibly ridiculous plan now.

"Keith has a T-ball game in thirty minutes that he said he and Lila will be at. I want to go over there and catch her in a conversation and, now that you're here, you can do your sneaky conversation bit to try and get to the bottom of her original deceit. A smooth operation considering the T-ball games are open to the public and you can say you were thinking about signing Bonnie up and that's why you're there."

Jones surprised her with a laugh.

She narrowed her eyes at him.

"What?"

"A 'smooth operation'? You sound very James Bond, is all."

Cassandra wasn't having it.

"I'm sure you could go through more official channels to talk to Lila—something you should do, James Bond–style or not, because she definitely lied—but I think a more casual approach might do everyone some good." Her gaze dropped to the cut that Jimmy had dealt Jones the night before. His button-up might be hiding it, but they both knew it was there. Maybe an unofficial questioning might work better on Lila.

When Cassandra looked back up, Jones was watching her with no more humor.

Instead the man appeared right tired.

"I wouldn't mind checking on Keith myself, anyway," he decided. "If we can get some answers while we're at it, then that works, too."

Cassandra clapped her hands together. Excitement flushed her cheeks with warmth. She wanted to get to the bottom of what had happened to stop it from ever happening again.

"Great! You're driving, right?" She opened her bag of fruit snacks and led him to the front door as he nodded. Cassandra stopped, house key raised in midair. "Wait. Did you need something? I mean, is that why you're here? Are you in the middle of work?"

A look she couldn't decipher crossed his face.

He shook his head.

"I came here to talk, but talking can happen anywhere so we're good."

Cassandra would have turned them right back around and sat down on the couch, ready to have any kind of conversation about their child and what that child would mean for the future. But she had already set herself in motion and wanted to see it through.

Plus, he was right. They could talk in the car about their situation just as easily as on a couch.

"So let's get this spy mission going before it gets too late," Jones added. "I promised Bonnie a nighttime story if I missed supper tonight."

Cassandra followed him out to what must have been his rental. She smiled as he opened the door for her and then waited until she was inside before closing it carefully behind her.

Jones Murphy was a gentleman. He had been one at the hotel months ago and that hadn't seemed to change now.

"The game is at the Woodland Complex near the entrance trail to Kintucket Woods," Cassandra began when Jones was seated beside her. "It's free admission and apparently something of a rivalry. Another boy from my class, Donavon, is on the team. The Winter Tigers."

"Now, *that* sounds like some kind of spy talk."

He pulled out of the neighborhood and had them driving a little bit before Cassandra's curiosity just couldn't hold anymore.

"You know, I spent a lot of today driving myself crazy about everything going on. Honestly, I even contemplated using my classroom's whiteboard to try to get my thoughts straight in my head. I didn't, of course, but I have to admit I don't know how any of you do it."

"Do it? You mean solve cases?"

"I mean any of it," she answered with genuine feeling. "It's not like all the bad keeps to a normal schedule or has a nighttime routine or curfew. I've felt constantly on edge and I was only wrapped up in this mess for less than a day."

Jones seemed to be considering his response.

"This job, any law-enforcement job, can be a lot. But sometimes that *a lot* can be a lot of good, too. That helps when the bad stacks up."

"I guess I can see that," she said. Cassandra decided to creep up to the point of conversation she'd been hoping to hit. She smoothed out the fabric of her dress over her thighs and tried to be gentle.

"It probably doesn't help the bad stack when The

Flood keeps getting brought up at almost every turn, even years later."

Jones stiffened.

He actually *stiffened*.

"I was wondering if you knew about that," he said. "I suppose it's hard not to here."

Some towns had endearing or odd stories that were detailed out by the locals.

Kelby Creek had corruption.

"June told me the local version of the story after I moved here. The man who hired me gave me an impassioned speech about how little ol' Kelby Creek was out of the past and looking to a brighter future. A few bad apples couldn't poison the orchard seemed to be his sticking point."

Jones snorted. It was a particularly nasty sound.

"It was more like the orchard was the poisoned part and the few apples were the only good."

He zipped up as soon as the last word left his mouth. Cassandra was outright staring at him. She turned her head and kept her gaze out the windshield.

But she didn't stop.

"Annie McHale," she said, reserving a good dose of awe for the name. "Kelby Creek's beginning of the end."

That got a look from the sheriff.

She tried to explain.

"It's what June told me once," she said. "That had Annie McHale not been kidnapped, the investigation into her wouldn't have uncovered all of the corruption. Her disappearance became the beginning of the end for the town. The downward slope."

"Well, jeez, that June sure is poetic."

"Don't worry, Sheriff." She reached out to pat his leg. It was an automatic move. Cassandra took her hand back as quickly as she'd touched him. She smiled at his glance over at her. "June was just as poetic about how, despite the inevitable end, there's been a growing light, too. Seems a lot of locals have lessened their stance against the sheriff's department in the last few years."

He took a turn and flipped on the headlights. The time change was plunging them deeper into darkness earlier every night. It's why the teeball games that had been added to the schedule for this time of year were played under floodlights. For now, it fit the mood in the car.

"Sheriff Chamblin, the one who hired most of the staff and is the reason why the department is still standing, told me that every bad moment in life will find a balance. All the betrayal, anger and pain... It'd be met later with some kind of cosmic reckoning." He snorted again. "Chamblin's a good man—smart, too—but I think it's too clean a thought to think every bad spot in your life is going to always find a good spot to make it better. Always waiting for the second shoe to drop is a tiring thing, and placing all of your hopes that it's going to be a good second shoe is downright cruel."

Cassandra had been after one question since she'd sat down, but now, she got caught in his double talk. Jones was saying something without saying it and she didn't know why.

"I only came back here to help my dad and now look at where we are," he continued, a good amount of loathing in his words. "Driving to a children's game in the hopes of finding out why a grown man attacked two kids and a pregnant woman, right before trying to figure out why after twenty years of good standing, a man decides to attack the law for some unknown and probably ridiculous reason."

She placed her hand on his leg and kept it there. This time Cassandra meant the contact.

The pressure seemed to still him.

She finally got around to her question, though she phrased it so he wouldn't have room not to answer.

"And, on top of all of that, you're reinvestigating Annie McHale's case."

The silence was profound.

And short.

Jones nodded.

"Something, I'm guessing by how sensitive the topic is, that's not public information," she added.

The man let out a long, low breath.

"No. It's not. Actually, only a few in the department even know I'm doing it." He shared a look with her. "And you."

She didn't smile but felt a warmth spread in her.

She shook it away quickly.

"That's why you think you're the connection to Bill at the school and being run off the road. And, well, Jimmy. Because you found out someone was lying about the original case."

He didn't look like he wanted to talk about work, yet he continued with no hesitation.

"You said June caught you up on the story of Kelby Creek, but how in-depth did she go about Annie?"

"Not too deep, I suppose. Annie was kidnapped by the sheriff at the time and the mayor. The FBI came in to help and one of their agents went missing, too, before her partner found the evidence that linked everyone together and then to years of corruption. Annie and the FBI agent were never found. The FBI came back and tried to weed out all of the corrupted in what everyone around here calls The Flood."

The sign for the Woodland Complex was lit up as they drove past it. The street that they followed in had several other cars making the trek to the different lots and fields inside. Despite her excitement to talk to Lila, though, Cassandra's attention was all on the sheriff.

"That's true but leaves out a lot of the gut punches. See, the timeline goes—Annie goes missing and the entire town bands together to look for her. Then the ransom call comes in asking for money in exchange for her. Sheriff Barkley, friend to the McHales and godfather to Annie, takes over. He decides to give backup to Annie's father at the exchange meeting at the park and, when the time comes, it turns out to be an ambush." His voice went flat. Cassandra searched his face for an emotion, but it was nothing but blank. He continued. "Several people were killed or hurt but the kidnappers didn't get the money, Annie's parents didn't get her. After that, the town's official website was hacked and a video recording of Annie tied up to a chair and bloody, crying for help, was uploaded to it. That's what went viral, that video. It's also what got the FBI's attention and brought

Agent James Delamere and Agent Jacqueline Ortega to our humble little town. They got to looking and then Agent Ortega went missing, too. But not before she left her partner a message saying she found a lead."

Jones was deep in his story but he still had the focus to pull them into a parking lot next to one of the fields. They were early, which was good.

Because Cassandra couldn't look away.

"Then, it started raining," he continued, putting the car in Park. "Then that rain turned into a flash flood and made the mayor hydroplane himself right into a ditch. By pure luck, the first person to come along the road was Agent Delamere. He went to help the unconscious mayor and, in doing so, accidentally found a necklace had come loose in the crash. The same necklace Annie had been wearing when she went missing. After that? Well, Agent Delamere started turning over those rocks and it led to a whole lot of other people in positions of power, until finally he needed backup to deal with all the snakes he'd found hidden beneath those rocks."

"That's why locals call the investigation into the corruption The Flood," she realized.

He nodded.

"It's the reason why the department has had to work so hard for redemption in the eyes of this town. It's why a lot of us couldn't stomach being around here right after the investigation ended."

Cassandra didn't know what to say to that, but she did come back to the original question.

"But something has happened since then to get you to go back over Annie's specific case?"

Jones let out another deep sigh.

"Annie doesn't just come from what was once the wealthiest family in Kelby Creek, she comes from the most beloved family in Kelby Creek," he said. "The entire town, for some unknown reason, just…loved them. When Annie went missing, we all looked for her. When we realized she was taken, we rallied alongside them. When they finally moved away after no leads or clues, we grieved with them. So when Annie's uncle was found to be involved in a human trafficking operation recently and his son testified against all of his father's bad without anyone being the wiser…it changed everything."

"If Annie's uncle had gone under the radar with his bad, then maybe the rest of the family had, too?"

It was a solid jump to make, easier for Cassandra, too, considering she hadn't been around to know the McHales. Definitely not to love them.

"That was the thought," he confirmed. "I started officially yesterday by going through the last day Annie was seen alive. Including all of the notes taken by everyone investigating the first time around. I wanted to step through Annie's every minute in the public if possible."

"That's where you found the lie."

Jones nodded.

"Annie spent the night before at Melinda Deacon's house, her neighbor and friend. The next morning she was seen walking across the acreage between the two houses to get home. Two people claimed to have spoken to her then—the Deacon gardener, Jeff King, and the Deacon maid, Vera Lohan. I spoke to Jeff yesterday to just confirm his earlier statement and, wouldn't you know it, he lost his top. Said there was no reason in the world to question him again. So I said I'd just move on to Vera. She's living in Huntsville now with her own business number so it's not hard."

He shook his head.

"Let me guess—Jeff the gardener didn't like that," Cassandra said.

"Nope. Yelled me out of the garden completely."

"So, naturally, you called Vera."

Jones chuckled.

"Yep. She also didn't want to talk but when I told her that the gardener had said the same thing, do you know what she said?"

Cassandra shook her head with bated breath.

"She said, 'What gardener?'"

Cassandra's bated breath turned into a surprised gasp.

"He lied, the gardener," she exclaimed. "Or, maybe she did."

"If she hadn't hung up on me, and then skirted my calls after, I would have kept pressing. Now I'm waiting for a call back from her daughter, who's still in town with her grandson. Maybe I can get her to open up a little to figure out what's going on."

Cassandra had pictured Vera as a younger woman, but if she had a daughter still in town and a grandson...

"Wait. Lohan. Her daughter's name isn't Jasmine, is it?"

Jones's eyes went wide. He nodded.

"Yeah, Jasmine Lohan."

A new wave of excitement went through Cassandra. She cut eye contact with Jones and surveyed the growing crowd of kids and adults on the brightly lit field and stands in front of them.

"I know this sounds wrong to say after everything, but, Sheriff Murphy, today might be your lucky day."

Cassandra saw the young boy with dark hair cropped close that she was looking for. Next to him was a woman holding a baby. Cassandra pointed.

"Because I have a Christopher Lohan in my class and he just so happens to be very good at T-ball."

Jones followed her gaze.

"Well, I'll be damned, that's Jasmine Lohan."

Christopher was waving frantically to another boy, who came walking up.

It was Keith.

"And I'll be damned by two," Cassandra said. "Because there's Lila Shaw."

Jones cracked a smirk.

His voice went a little deep when he met Cassandra's gaze.

It did something to her that was wholly inappropriate in the moment, but she was more than game for what he said next.

"Well, Miss West, looks like our night is about to get interesting."

Chapter Ten

The kids went to the field after the coaches. The rest went to either the stands on the other side of the fence, or the lawn behind them. Everyone could still see and it was that everyone whom Jones tried to avoid as they walked up to Jasmine Lohan, the maid's daughter.

"She might not be happy to see me if her mom got to her after my call," Jones warned Cassandra with a whisper near her ear as they were walking. "If she gets to fussing, you might need to give us space."

Cassandra, who was all energy now, shrugged.

"She might not be happy to see you because you're the sheriff, but I'm the one teaching her son how to read. She might fuss at you, but she's not fussing at me."

Jones couldn't help himself. He chuckled.

"Miss West, if I didn't know any better I'd think you're having fun."

Cassandra laughed.

"On a normal night I'm looking at craft supplies, lesson plans and a bedtime of eight, where I just lie around and try to get comfortable. So, yes, I might be a *little* enthused for a livelier existence right now."

Jones didn't want to, but he imagined Cassandra in bed, pregnant and alone. It was the first image that popped into his head and he abruptly made it leave.

He needed to focus.

Cassandra was already there.

She quickened her pace and met Jasmine before he could. She was all smiles and warmth when the other woman took them in.

"Hi there, Jasmine," she said in greeting. She went to the baby in the sling next. "And this must be little Oliver. Boy, aren't you growing!"

Jasmine took the bombardment in stride. Her lips stretched into a smile when she realized who Cassandra was.

"Miss West! Hey! How are you doing? You come out to watch the game?"

Cassandra had told him in the car that she tried to have a relationship with all of her kids' parents, but Jasmine had never been too chatty at school functions or meetings. That was okay, she'd reasoned, since some parents didn't even show up, but she still wasn't sure how far her presence would go when he started asking questions.

"I'm actually here to check up on Keith," Cassandra admitted, which was partly true.

Jasmine immediately was sympathetic. She nodded knowingly.

"I still can't believe what happened. You know, Bill used to be one of my mom's clients and she said nothing but nice things about him. Kristine said as much, too, when we were talking at lunch today."

Cassandra's eyes widened. Not enough to be terribly noticeable, but when she looked at Jones he understood the meaning of what she was trying to convey.

They didn't have to force a segue to talking about Vera. Jasmine had just done it naturally seconds into their conversation.

"I truly hate that the kids had to go through that, but I'm sure glad this one here was able to come in and save us before things got any worse." Cassandra did an almost talk-show-host type of hand sweep toward him. "I don't know if you two have met, but this is Bonnie's dad, Jones Murphy."

Jasmine had all the markings of a nice, pleasant woman who was schooled in the ways of Southern politeness. She was going through the motions of someone about to accommodate a stranger—her smile stretched, her hand started to rise—but then, like Jimmy had flipped at the interrogation table, she changed the instant she registered his name.

Her smile was gone when Jasmine met Jones's eyes.

"You mean, *Sheriff* Jones Murphy."

Cassandra must have caught on to the change.

And she didn't like it.

"Now, Jasmine, I need you to take that tone and flush it," she said sharply. "Flush it right on down. There's no need for it here."

Jasmine was as surprised as Jones at the admonishment. Jones readied himself for a prickly response, but Cassandra had been right. Jasmine wasn't going to fuss at her.

"Mama already told me this one here was bothering her today," she told Cassandra with a notably more respectful tone. Jasmine kept eye contact with Jones, however. "I'm not going to help him drag her back into the black hole that is this town's awful past. Just because some of us won't move on, doesn't mean all of us have to be stuck."

Her eyes narrowed.

She'd meant that comment specifically for him.

Too bad he'd heard worse.

"I'm just trying to figure out some things that need figuring out," he defended. "That's all. I'm not trying to drag anyone into any kind of black hole."

Jasmine crossed her arms over her baby. The movement didn't wake him, but it did show Jones that he wasn't going to get anywhere with her. She was physically closing him off without saying the words.

"If the FBI and a slew of other law enforcement didn't figure it out, I'm not betting on your horse there, *Sheriff*."

Frustration came up like bad heartburn. Jones understood the distrust in Kelby Creek law just as much as he loathed it. He couldn't do his job if he couldn't even get people to answer one question without pushback.

He was about to say as much when a soft hand took his.

Just like that the frustration ebbed.

Jones looked down at Cassandra's smile. Out of focus beneath it was her pregnant belly.

"Hey, Jones? I see Keith's mama over there. Maybe it would be a good time to go see how she's doing, too." Cassandra squeezed his hand. "I'll stay here and keep Jasmine and this adorable kiddo company in the meantime."

Jones lost his words.

For a lot of reasons.

He didn't want her to be alone with Jasmine because he knew, deep down, that she'd get the woman to talk. It's what he wanted, what he was trying for, but involving Cassandra? He didn't like that.

But then he felt the warmth of her hand. *Really* felt it.

Jones was amazed that it calmed him without any effort.

He was also amazed that he stepped back and took her subtle directive.

He nodded to both women.

"I think that's a mighty fine idea."

Cassandra let go of him.

Jones flexed his hand.

It felt as wrong as walking away from her.

CASSANDRA WATCHED HIM until it was clear that Lila was more welcoming than Jasmine had been to the man. She also gave some time to the woman at her side, so when Jasmine spoke again, there was a calmer tenor to her voice.

"I didn't realize you were friendly with the sheriff," she said. "I actually didn't realize the sheriff was friendly with anyone anymore."

Cassandra was only a little bit uncomfortable. The sheriff had been plenty friendly with her at every turn, but it wasn't her place to correct her.

"He's a good man," Cassandra said. "And he means what he says. He's just trying to help."

Jasmine huffed.

Baby Oliver moved at the sound but didn't wake.

"Everyone always says that, you know? 'He's a good man.' Like that's some kind of magic phrase that makes strangers trustworthy all of a sudden. 'He's a good man.' We thought Bill was a good man. We thought a lot of people were good men and women before him. I'm sure someone even told you the same thing about the sheriff. 'He's a good man, Cassandra West.' Now look at you, coming to my child's T-ball game with some attempt to what? Get me to convince my mother to talk to him about something she doesn't want to talk about? I know you're not a local, but those of us who are don't look at the badge the same way you do. 'He's a good man' just isn't going to cut it."

Cassandra hadn't expected the amount of passion that Jasmine had forced out of every word. But maybe she should have. Jones had the same intensity to his words when he spoke of Annie McHale.

Cassandra was also sure of something else.

There was something Jasmine wasn't saying that she could have been.

"Do you know why I teach kindergarten?"

The words came out before Cassandra realized where she wanted to go with them.

How could she expect Jasmine to ever possibly open up if she didn't?

"My mom left my family when I was six," Cassandra continued, not that Jasmine had tried to answer. "I used to think one of the worst things she could have done was leave without saying goodbye. That waking up one day and her just not being there was a pain that my little mind couldn't handle. But, then I got older."

Cassandra smiled. She felt it and she knew exactly what it looked like. Quiet, barely there. Sad but with some peace to it. Sorry that she was sharing something painful, even if it didn't necessarily hurt the person she was sharing it with.

"See, it took me a while to realize that the worst thing my mother ever did for me was announce that she was leaving before she did," she continued. "I was six and *that* announcement became a core memory very quickly. It was like she was reading a grocery list that she'd already read several times. There were a lot of reasons she was going, but there was only one that really stuck with me."

It was like it was yesterday, hearing her mother speak in the living room next to the front door. Her father, so shocked he was quiet as he stood next to her.

"She said I was too much to handle," Cassandra explained simply. "Said she wasn't built for small children. That I would be better without her even trying. That way, I didn't feel her failure later."

"That's cruel." Jasmine's voice was quiet, but she was correct.

Cassandra agreed with a nod.

"It also followed me, in every choice I ever made. I was terrified of biting off more than I could chew and I was just so sure that having children was too much to chew. I mean, if it was for her, it had to be for me."

Jasmine not so subtly looked at Cassandra's pregnant belly.

"But then, that part of me that was resentful and angry at her for years started to show up. I still didn't want children, but then I started to wonder if I could teach them instead. And not just kids, but the same age my mother couldn't handle. It was a dare to myself, and a way to prove that I could do what she couldn't. So I became a kindergarten teacher and, well, it changed everything. Now, look at me—I'm pregnant and I'm not watching how much I chew."

Cassandra was surprised at herself. She'd only ever told that story to one other person and he had died in a car accident before she even had the chance to tell him that she was considering having children with him.

"That's a nice story," Jasmine said, also clearly taken aback by the share. "But why are you telling me this now?"

Cassandra pointed to Jones.

"Because seven months ago, I listened to that man anguish over whether or not he should run for sheriff. No part of him wanted to come back to Kelby Creek, but when his father got hurt he did. He left a life he never thought he'd leave behind and came back to the one place in all the world he didn't want to come back to. He sacrificed because he was asked to, because he said he was needed, because a good great part of that man wanted to undo years of anger, resentment and pain. Because he *is* a good man, Jasmine, even if the phrase is overused. He came back to help. But he can't do it alone."

That was as good as she was going to be able to give in the way of trying to convince Jasmine to talk. A vulnerable story and the truth about the man behind the badge.

Sure, she didn't know him that well objectively, but, as sappy as it sounded, Cassandra really felt like she *knew* him.

That she had for a while.

She placed her hand on her belly and thought about their son.

Jasmine was quiet. The game started after the sound of the whistle being blown. Parents and spectators cheered. Cassandra suddenly felt tired. Jones was still talking to Lila, but she couldn't read either one's body language.

Baby Oliver made a soft coo in his sleep.

It served as a way to break the silence.

"I'm only going to say this once and after that you, the sheriff and anyone with a badge will leave me and my family alone about this. Understood?"

Cassandra nodded. She was relieved that her speech had resonated.

"Your goodhearted sheriff there was asking about the morning before Annie went missing, about my mother's original statement. And about some gardener who had given one, too." Jasmine shook her head. "The gardener was never scheduled the same day as my mother. If he was there, he wasn't on schedule."

"He lied, then."

"He wasn't the only one." Jasmine chewed on her lip, and she seemed to really consider her next words carefully. "I thought I'd take this to the grave. Mom would have, too, but her memory…well, it isn't what it used to be." Jasmine did a quick look around them. Cassandra leaned in. "Annie didn't leave the Deacon house alone that morning. Someone was with her."

Jasmine's entire demeanor changed. Like she was closing in on herself. Like she was lost.

Cassandra had to egg her on.

"Who?"

Jasmine's answer was so quiet, Cassandra barely heard her.

"Me." She turned to look Cassandra right in the eye. "And we didn't go to her house when we left."

Her words came out in a rush after that. She told Cassandra something she herself claimed she had never told another soul other than her mother. Cassandra made sure to burn every sentence into her memory. She wanted her recap to be perfect for Jones, because she knew there was no way Jasmine was ever going to repeat herself again.

When Jasmine was finished, Cassandra thanked her from the bottom of her heart. Yet, the woman looked far from happy.

"My mother was protecting me when she chose to keep all of that a secret and I've kept that secret, just like you will about my involvement, to protect my family," she said. "I know why I did what I did and I stand by it. But I can't claim to know why everyone does what they do. Neither can you, great teacher or not. So let me be maybe the first person to tell you about that man." She nodded toward Jones and Lila. "He might've come back for his father, but he didn't take the mantle of sheriff to do good in Kelby Creek."

Jasmine's voice hardened. They were past whatever amicable connection they'd had. There was nothing but warning in what she said next.

"Believe you me, Jones Murphy only came back to town for revenge."

Chapter Eleven

Jones glanced over his shoulder. Cassandra and Jasmine seemed to be okay. They were talking and Cassandra didn't look to be upset. Not that he knew what exactly it was that she did when something had her going. Well, other than at the department, when he refused to go rest. She'd gone from polite to pulsing pretty fast. Then she'd just gone all together.

Now, though, she looked to be okay. Open and a small smile across her lips.

Jones wanted to keep his gaze on her for a little longer, but Lila Shaw had finally decided to drop the heys, hellos and how-do-you-dos and address his presence head on.

"Keith told that teacher of his about Bill," she said outright. "Didn't he?"

Jones wasn't going to betray the little man's involvement, but he was going to stick to the whole admitting-it thing.

"It's a small town, Lila, you know how news travels," he said, sidestepping. "And how when you don't want it moving, it only travels all the faster."

Lila dropped her chin a little, defeated. Or, really, it looked more like she was tired.

"Having a relationship with someone isn't a crime," she said.

"No, but lying to law enforcement is."

She sighed. Everyone had been sighing a lot lately it seemed. Everyone was tired. Everyone wanted things like this in Kelby Creek to end. Everyone wanted some kind of peace they weren't getting.

But Lila had lied about an attack against children and a pregnant woman, and if she didn't tell him the truth now, he definitely was going to be the opposite of her peace.

Jones was about to start in, thinking she'd already caved, but Lila surprised him. She spoke bluntly.

"I started seeing Bill after running into him at the bar one night. He was nice and funny and, I don't know, it worked. That was back in February. Joel was gone on his trucking route for weeks at a time then. I wasn't a fan of that, but, well, communication has never been our strong suit, so instead I guess I turned to Bill." She paused, looking lost for a moment. Jones wasn't going to press just yet. Not if she was willing to keep right on talking.

Lila ran a hand through her hair. Her words were drenched in regret.

"It was a casual thing at first, me and Bill, but a few weeks ago he started talking about being with me. Full time, no hiding. Said we could leave town together and start over, happy." She snorted. "I told him the truth that happy doesn't fit everyone, and plus, I couldn't leave Keith. Not when he's in the middle of looking for a forever family. It's not his fault that I'm broken, you know?"

Jones's ears had already perked up.

"When did you tell Bill that you wouldn't leave without Keith?"

That's where the regret was.

She'd unknowingly given Bill an obstacle to his happiness.

Now, though, Jones could tell she realized it.

"Last week."

They let that sit for a second.

"I didn't know what he was planning—I guess I still don't—but I never should have used Keith as an excuse. It wasn't fair to the boy...and it wasn't fair to your kid, who had to go through that, too. I'm sorry, Sheriff. I really am."

"You aren't Bill, Lila. I'm not going to blame you for what he decided to do or try to do. You should have told me, though. Would have saved us some head scratching."

She nodded.

Someone on the field hit the ball and sent it flying. Parents and visitors alike stood tall, whooping and hollering.

Jones didn't need more from Lila, but he didn't want to leave her yet, either. He looked back over his shoulder again. Cassandra was still talking to Jasmine. She was rubbing her belly.

Jones felt a whole lot at the sight.

He cleared his throat and tried to put some of that feeling to good.

"You know, Lila, broken people can be happy again. It might not be the way we thought it would happen, but maybe that's what makes it work. We don't see it coming so we can't worry about it, just enjoy it when it happens."

Lila blew out another breath. This time it wobbled.

Jones softened even more.

"I'm sure you and Joel can work this out. Find a way to maybe start again."

The woman was crying now. Not hard, but he saw a tear streak down her cheek. It alarmed him.

However, not as much as when she turned to face him full on.

Lila Shaw was angry.

"Joel and I can't start again," she growled. "We never started because *he* wasn't who I was supposed to be with."

Jones liked to think he did a fairly good job of keeping up with the details, but that one had him pause.

"I don't understand," he admitted.

Lila laughed. It was harsh and pointed.

"Of all of the people to forget about them, I didn't think it would be you."

Lila… Breckinridge.

Jones remembered her maiden name a split second before he made the connection he should have already made.

"Max," he said.

Jones hadn't forgotten about Max, Detective Juliet's

brother. A young man who'd left town after The Flood only to die in a car crash a few months later.

What he *hadn't* connected together was Max's girlfriend at the time was one Lila Breckinridge. Now Lila Shaw.

"Max," Lila repeated, but with a world more of a feeling. "The love of my life, the man I wanted to spend forever with. Did you know that he asked me to leave town with him, too? He did. He said he'd pack me up himself if I wanted." Lila's shoulders drooped. More tears followed down her cheeks. A woman near them turned around to look, but was quick to avert her gaze.

Lila continued, uncaring of a potential audience.

"But, what did I say? Not yet. Not yet because my mother was so *heartbroken* about what happened in this damn town that she quit her job at the hospital in protest. That she conveniently forgot about bills and health insurance and future employers all over a principled stand against the big, bad corruption. And do you know what that got her in the end, Sheriff? Nothing. Nothing but debt and a daughter who had to stay around to try and get the finances fixed before she could go be with the man she loved and *start a new life*. And what did that get me? A funeral, a loveless marriage and absolute rage at the fact that I'm still stuck in this awful town."

She was all-out crying now.

The woman who had turned earlier was now clearly listening. Jones tried to readjust his stance to give Lila more privacy.

Which didn't matter much when the woman took a deep breath. Followed by another one. The crying lessened, and her words were clear.

Though, they would have hurt regardless, if they were in between sobs or not.

Lila met his eye.

"Why couldn't you see they were bad?"

Silence.

It flooded between them.

Lila didn't have to explain her question. She didn't have to say anything anymore.

Jones knew what she meant.

He'd asked himself the same thing.

Why hadn't he known the sheriff was an evil man? Why hadn't he picked up on the backroom dealings? The cover-ups? The cold cases growing faster than they ever should have? The plot to ransom Annie McHale?

Why hadn't he seen the bad?

If he had, their world would have been much different.

He could have protected everyone.

Annie. Max.

Helen.

But he hadn't.

Jones wrapped his arm around Lila's shoulders.

He said the only thing he could.

"I'm sorry."

He wasn't sure if she could forgive him, but Lila let him hold her steady while she went back to crying.

They stood there for a few minutes like that.

This time around Jones didn't turn around and look for Cassandra.

He looked ahead instead, but all he saw was the past.

THE CAR RIDE out of the Woodland Complex was, the best Cassandra could describe it, strained.

Jones had slid into the driver's seat with a quietness that had been loud in its own way. He'd sat straighter, yet seemed to be dragging downward.

Exhausted wasn't the right word.

Cassandra wondered if the same could be said about her.

After her mission was a success, Jasmine had continued to talk about the past until Jones had ended his conversation with Lila.

It hadn't been about Kelby Creek.

It *had* been about Jones Murphy.

And his late wife, Helen.

Cassandra had never asked about Bonnie's mother, about his romantic life in general. There had never been the place or the right time. He hadn't asked her, either. It wasn't like they'd been living distraction-free, after all. The last two days' problems could have filled two years' worth of stress, as far as Cassandra was concerned.

Still, she'd known logically that the sheriff might have been a widower, just as he might have been divorced.

Cassandra had never once thought that his wife had been killed.

Caught in the cross fire at the ambush during Annie McHale's ransom exchange.

Cassandra could have cried on the spot for how awful her heart hurt for the man. No wonder he'd left Kelby Creek to start a new life with Bonnie.

How had he had the strength to come back?

And not only come back, but also reinvestigate the case that had led to his wife's death?

"Sometimes singing praise for finding justice is just noise to hide the fact that you're really looking for revenge," Jasmine had said before Cassandra had said goodbye. "Don't get caught in the cross fire, too."

Cassandra hadn't liked the phrasing, and she also didn't like how the warning had made her feel. She tried to push away those thoughts as she and Jones shared what they had learned.

"Jasmine and Annie had become friends after Vera took Jasmine to work with her a few times while Annie was visiting," she explained after recapping the two lies told in the original investigation. "They spent the night at the Deacon house, but the next morning they were woken up by Vera instead of her watching Annie walk to her house. She wanted to make sure they didn't miss their study slot at the library."

Jones, who in silhouette still seemed impossibly big behind the car's wheel, cocked his head to the side in question.

"Their study slot?"

"It's for one of the two rooms in the back of Redman Library, you know, the public one near downtown. You can reserve them for studying or meetings or just to read without any interruptions."

"And Annie and Jasmine signed up to study that morning?"

His eyes stayed ahead on the road so Cassandra made sure to say no instead of just shaking her head.

"No. Jasmine said that Annie had been going once

a week to the library to read this one book series she'd become obsessed with, but knew her parents would flip out if they found out she'd checked them out. That morning Jasmine said Annie reserved the room as soon as it opened at eight, which was a little weird since she typically did it in the afternoons. Jasmine didn't think anything of it, though, but admitted books weren't her thing and Jasmine left her there to go to her boyfriend's place, where she went back to sleep for a few hours. She didn't have any plans to meet Annie later. They only really hung out after bumping into each other or at the library when Jasmine had the time."

Jones shook his head and growled.

"According to her parents, Annie was in her room from seven twenty in the morning until nine ten in the morning. Not the library."

Cassandra shrugged.

"Maybe she lied to them and they didn't know? According to Jasmine, she wasn't even sure they knew she was friends with Annie. No one came to question her after Annie went missing. Her mother was only questioned because she was on schedule with the Deacons. Oh, and speaking of the schedule, according to it the gardener shouldn't have been there. Jasmine couldn't explain that, said her mother couldn't, either."

Jones was back to shaking his head.

"Why didn't any of this come up the first time around?"

It was a rhetorical question. The corruption in the department was the answer.

Cassandra tried to answer it, anyway.

"Vera thought she was protecting herself and her daughter by taking them out of the picture. It sounds like she only dropped the facade on the phone with you because she's having issues with her memory due to old age. Or else I'm pretty sure all of that would still be locked up tight based on how much Jasmine didn't want to talk about it now."

"But she did," Jones pointed out. "She told you."

Cassandra waved off his comment.

"Honestly, I think she needed to get it off of her chest."

Cassandra expected some follow-up questions.

She didn't get any.

"Lila confirmed she had an affair with Bill," he said after a moment. "We talked a little more and I think Bill was trying to take Keith so they could all leave town together. At least, that's my hope. I'll get Foster to follow up with Bill, but my guess is that, for once, a coincidence in Kelby Creek was actually a coincidence. I don't think Bill at the school was connected to my look into Annie's case."

"Do you think Jimmy used Bill's name to try and throw you off?"

Jones nodded.

"I think he did it to make me waste some time. I just don't know why."

The drive to the Woodland Complex had felt like a good stretch of time. The drive back to Cassandra's house felt like a blink.

Suddenly she was staring at her front door, standing on the welcome mat and the sheriff towering behind her.

She unlocked the door and stepped inside with a little heat in her cheeks.

They hadn't had a lot of time to be alone together, at least not with a mystery to solve pressing down on them.

Now?

Now it could be the two of them, finally talking.

Cassandra dropped her keys in her catchall and waited for the door to shut behind them.

It didn't.

She turned to find Jones still on the welcome mat.

He looked more exhausted than before.

Cassandra knew then that he wasn't going to come inside.

"We've been going a mile a minute and I know part of that is on me and me alone," he began the second she found his dark eyes on her. "I want to talk, I really want to talk, about everything. About you, about me and about our son, but right now I need to go back to the department and I can't take you there with me."

Jones took a startlingly quick step forward. Before she could take him all in, he was a breath away. He bent down enough that his words were closer and not lost in their height difference.

"But I want to tell you right now that, in no uncertain terms, I want to be a part of this child's life. I want to and will be a father to him, and do whatever I can and whatever you want me to, to see that happen. You don't have to worry about that or question me ever about that. I will love him like I love Bonnie. With everything I have."

Cassandra might have melted at that admission.

She might have cried or kissed him, whichever struck her fancy first.

Yet, as much as she heard the sincerity in his words, she also heard the *but* coming next.

"But, as much as I may want to say otherwise, I can't be with you. Not like we were before we both came back to town. I don't even know if that's something you'd want, but I wanted to go ahead and let you know that it's something that I can't have. I'm sorry."

He took a step back, left no room for her to respond and was back out on the porch in another blink.

"Thank you for tonight, Cassandra. I really mean it."

Jones gave her a small smile, a quick nod and then was gone.

Cassandra watched his taillights disappear down the street, Jasmine's words of warning blaring in her mind.

Chapter Twelve

He saw her there.

In the crowd.

She was wearing a thick jacket and her hair was shorter. A different color, too. But he knew it was her.

What he didn't know was why she was there.

Why she was watching the sheriff so closely.

He half expected her to go to the man, to try and warn him. Or scare him away. Given her moods, she could go either way.

But she didn't approach the sheriff. She just watched him and then watched him and the teacher as they walked back to their car.

It wasn't until they were off and gone that she went, too.

She was casual but she was careful.

She'd have to be by now.

He blew out a breath after her car was a pair of tail-lights in the distance. He couldn't see his breath in the air, but the forecast called for much colder weather in the coming days. He liked fall in Kelby Creek. The storms were much less frequent.

"It's done."

Dark hair and a sweet voice took up the space to his left. Jasmine Lohan wasn't smiling. The man on his right stayed quiet. They were all standing at the edge of the field, the sound of children yelling and playing ever present.

"I told them the truth," she added. There was bite to her words. She didn't like helping him.

She didn't have a choice, though.

Her mother's jumbling thoughts had become a problem. If she hadn't helped him, well, then there would be another victim of Kelby Creek's past.

And she didn't want that.

Hell, neither did he.

But that didn't mean he wouldn't continue to be proactive.

"That's good," he said. "Now your part is done."

Jasmine might not have been happy to have been tangled together with him, but she'd stopped herself when given the chance to leave. He could tell she was looking out at the field. Looking at her young son, while wearing her second.

He'd never thought Jasmine the type to be a mother. She'd never liked commitment. She'd proclaimed that loudly and often. Then again, she hadn't married her partner. So maybe she'd compromised with herself.

One commitment instead of another.

"I only came to you so the sheriff could find out about Annie's *other* life in a more organic way," he reminded her. "You told the truth, which is what I wanted.

Everything else—" he found her son on the field, running between two bases "—is fine now."

Jasmine was noticeably relieved.

But she still stuck to her spot.

"How did you know they'd come here tonight?"

"When no one talks at the department, it's because
they're out gossiping." He shrugged. "I knew once he
talked to your mother, you'd be next in line. Since he
doesn't want everything he's doing out in the public,
coming here to see you was a possibility I thought might
pan out. If it hadn't, well, there were other ways to get
the information to him. Though, I'm glad we didn't
have to resort to them."

That did it.

Jasmine was done with him.

She nodded and walked away. Jasmine was a loyal
friend but a more loyal daughter. However, he suspected
being a mother trumped those two for the woman.

Using her sons would have done the trick if needed.

The man at his side made a noise.

He was grumpy.

He always was.

"You guessed the sheriff might show up," he said,
voice low and the epitome of being annoyed. "But you
had no idea he'd bring the teacher."

It wasn't a question.

"No, I had no idea he'd bring the teacher," he admitted. "I also had no idea he'd rely on her to question
someone about Annie."

He stretched tall and wide.

He was bored now.

"Let's keep an eye on them, see what they do next."

"They're going to go to the library. That's what they'll do next if Jasmine told them right."

He didn't like the man's know-it-all tone.

He rolled his eyes.

"They can go to that library every day for a year and it won't do them any good if they can't find out what Annie was up to."

"What if they don't? Or, what if they do?" The other man followed him as he walked around the crowd and headed toward their car. "I know you're all 'big picture' with plans, but the rest of us would feel a lot better if you at least gave us an idea of what to expect next."

He let another breath out, becoming more bored by the second.

"If they don't then we'll have to find a way to get them where we want them," he said simply. "If they do, well, that's when I make a phone call."

He had to turn to see the other man's eyes widen in realization.

"This is too complicated," he objected. "It's too much. Can't we just leave? Can't we disappear and just live out the rest of our days happy, healthy and not behind bars or dead?"

He shook his head.

He wasn't leaving.

Not now, not ever.

"This is my town." He had his car door open. He paused before settling inside. "No one is making me leave. Not the sheriff, not his teacher friend, not you and certainly not *her*."

The man went quiet.

Which was good because there wasn't a thing he could say to make him change his mind.

Kelby Creek was his.

And he was about to make sure everyone within its town limits knew that.

A WEEK WENT BY.

One full week of no word from Jones, no mention in the news of his attacker being caught or even identified and not even a whisper of Annie McHale's second investigation.

It was driving Cassandra batty.

Not to mention, playing havoc on her emotions.

One day she cried, a lot. Another day she was angry and fussed at almost every inanimate object in her house, including an Amazon package from her father. It had a baby-naming book inside along with a blanket covered in sailboats.

She said some curses at it after wondering if Jones had a boy name he was fond of.

That anger came with some self-reflection, but only a day later.

It was *great* that Jones wanted to be in his son's life.

It was *fine* that Jones didn't want to be anything other than a co-parent with her.

She was *good* with both of these things and hadn't expected to rekindle any kind of relationship with him after their surprise reunion.

Sure, had she fantasized about being wrapped in his

arms or listening to his deep monotone as he talked to her in the last seven months?

Absolutely.

Did that mean that she wanted to be his—his, what?—girlfriend?

His wife?

Cassandra decided to bury any and all questions about her feelings deep down until a later date.

She spent the next few days instead focusing all of her energy on Annie McHale.

And the Redman Library.

It was on Saturday morning Cassandra put on her maternity jeans and her least conspicuous blouse, and went to the library by herself. She wasn't sure if Jones had done the same already, but it was such an odd clue that she couldn't stand wondering about it any longer.

Redman Library was one of the few public spaces in Kelby Creek that hadn't received some kind of funding, donation or gift from the McHale family's fortune through the years. That made Annie's dedication to its study rooms all the more interesting. Doubling that interest was the fact that Annie had already graduated high school and hadn't yet enrolled in college. If she had been going to a study room merely to read, the material wasn't for school.

Why go to a public space for privacy when you're the wealthiest heir in Kelby Creek, Cassandra thought as she mounted the four steps up to the front doors. It wasn't the first time she'd wondered. Even if the material she was reading was scandalous, at least scandalous enough to want to keep it from her parents, then surely she could find somewhere else to read it?

"Hi there!"

A chirp of greeting came from a young man behind the front desk. Cassandra recognized him. He'd substituted at the school before, usually in music class.

Cassandra sidled up to the desk, polite smile coming alive.

The main reading room opened up to their right. Tables and chairs were placed at random throughout the space, making way for themed book stands and endcaps. Cassandra hadn't been there in a long while but remembered the layout well enough. The children's room was located in the back left corner. The study rooms were located along the back wall. Neither door could be seen from the main room unless you walked through the nonfiction stacks toward the back.

If Annie had wanted privacy to read whatever she was reading, reserving one of the rooms was definitely the ticket.

"Hey, there, Lloyd," she said. "I didn't realize you were working at Redman."

Lloyd was wonderful with children but terrible at confrontation. Cassandra had once seen him bullied by a fourth grader so she could see why he'd be more comfortable out of the classroom.

He was also too young to have been at Redman during Annie's original visits.

Lloyd started to laugh but then caught himself. He looked over at two men sitting at the computer bay near the middle of the room. They didn't appear to be offended by his burst of noise.

"Lady, I've been here for over a year now." He leaned over the counter, all dramatic. "And apparently you've missed my career news and I've missed your expecting news?"

Cassandra felt her cheeks heat.

It was amazing how, even in such a small town, she was still managing to run in to people who were so shocked to find her pregnant.

"I guess we both did." Cassandra rubbed a hand over her stomach. "Six and a half months along, baby boy, cravings include Doritos, but only the Cool Ranch flavor."

Lloyd laughed in good humor.

"So, basically, Baby Boy has good taste."

Cassandra shared in the mirth.

"I suppose so."

Lloyd settled back into his chair.

"Does this mean you got married, too, and I wasn't invited?" He looked to her hand. No ring. His smile fell a little. "Or, am I being too nosy into something that has nothing to do with my body or life?"

If Lloyd had been someone else, say Coach Rich, who had asked almost every time he saw her who the father was despite her open desire to keep that to herself for the time being, Cassandra might have gone the defensive route. But she liked Lloyd. He was one of the few people she'd known who truly enjoyed helping children.

Cassandra also was, admittedly, more in her emotions than normal lately.

Either way she responded without worrying about spending the next few minutes dodging more and more questions.

"His father is a wonderful man but we're just friends," she said. "Baby Boy was a bit of a surprise."

Cassandra made sure to show that she wasn't at all put out by the situation. Lloyd picked up on her mood.

"Well, can I just say you're absolutely glowing," he said. "And I'm not just saying that because that's what most people say in lieu of an actual compliment."

Cassandra laughed.

"Thank you, I'll take it."

Lloyd seemed pleased with himself. He opened the door to the real reason she was there.

"So what can I help you with this fine Saturday morning?"

Cassandra had already rehearsed this part in the car. She tried to keep her request casual.

"I'm actually thinking about renting the study rooms for a few tutoring sessions I'll be doing next year after school. I wanted to go ahead and get the logistics down before baby here comes and I get lost in bottles and diapers on top of lesson plans and my planner. Do you think I could check them out now? Are they in use?"

It wasn't a total lie but it wasn't the total truth. Cassandra was often asked if she was open for extra tutoring during the school year, but she usually took those at the coffee shop or at school, given the time of need. She also had already decided to leave tutoring off her docket for the current school year since she had to believe she'd still be getting used to the balance of teaching kids and finally having one live with her.

Lloyd was unsuspecting of her half-truth. It made her feel even more guilty when he nodded profusely.

"You know those rooms have been pretty popular this week. I had to chase a couple of teens making out away from one, and then a few other people wanted to see if we were like Hogwarts or something and had the forbidden books hidden in them. Then there was the actual sheriff who came in on Tuesday, asking about using one of the rooms for a party for his kid." He laughed. "I had to remind every single person that this is a *library* and all the study rooms are for studying, hence the name."

He shook his head. She made sure to control her expression.

So Jones had already been there to check out the rooms. He'd also apparently done the same as her and kept his real curiosity out of the request.

Had he found something there?

Was it pointless for her to go look now?

Cassandra didn't know what her eyes could do that Jones's couldn't, but she decided she had to try or it would drive her anxiousness through the proverbial roof.

"Before I take a look, how do you reserve the space, anyway? Do I need to fill out a form or something?" she asked.

"I wish," Lloyd said with a sigh. "We're not that organized. We just enter the request in a log. Paper records. Can you imagine? I'm trying to convince them to digitalize that system. There are tons of scheduling apps for free, you know? We'll get there."

Paper records. That meant there was a written log somewhere of who signed out the study rooms, and Cassandra thought she might know who had the older ones.

She let Lloyd give her the short directions to the first study room and thanked him twice.

When she made her way to the door, passing by four stacks of old and severely used books, Cassandra couldn't shake a new, creeping feeling.

Despite no one being around, she felt the rising sensation that someone was watching her.

But why would anyone do that?

It wasn't like she knew anything important. It wasn't like *she* was important.

She shook her head at the silly thought and opened the first study-room door.

Had she known just how wrong she was, she would have never gone into that room.

But she had no idea what was going to happen.

So she shut the door behind her and tried her best to think like Annie McHale.

Chapter Thirteen

Jones grunted.

He readjusted, trying to get comfortable.

He grunted again.

He couldn't move from his seat and that was starting to really grate against his nerves.

"Watch it," he told his captor.

She did nothing with the warning. The cold hit his foot like a slap to the face.

"Bonnie," Jones yelled out. "I told you that you could paint my toenails only if you didn't touch my toes with those freezing little-kid hands of yours."

Bonnie, sitting beneath his desk, let out a devious cackle.

"It's not my fault your feet are so big! It's hard *not* to touch them."

Jones rolled his eyes as his father let out a burst of laughter from the hallway.

"She's got a point there," he said, appearing in the doorway. "And may I just say that when she did my nails? No issues whatsoever with the size of my feet."

Jones couldn't see Bonnie, but he felt her nod.

"Yep, yep!"

Jones lifted his eyes from the notes on his desk. They were in his father's office, which was filled with spillover from the hardware store he owned. Ever since Jones had convinced his father to become partners with his longtime employee, some of his dad's free time had become dedicated to trying to figure out which hobbies he truly liked. That pursuit somehow had turned into a lot of random things finding their way into both the hardware store and their home.

Plus a storage room, which Jones visited more than he liked.

Right now the three of them were in close proximity to a desk covered in sheriff-department files, a cabinet filled with the miniature planes, most half-painted, and a bookcase that held more how-to manuals for various hobbies than probably most stores had in stock.

Then there was what Bonnie added to the mix, which, at the moment, included a manicure-and-pedicure set she was using on Jones's feet.

"Better my big feet than that thing you call a nose," he told his father with a grin. "We're almost at funding for the K-9 unit at the department. Maybe you should apply?"

It was a joke and it landed.

His father laughed.

"Remind me in a few years when you realize your nose finally matches mine."

Jones waved his father to the lone seat across from them. The chair was upholstered in a floral print that was dark and busy. It had been his mother's favorite and one of the few things that had followed him through every move he'd made after she passed away when he was twenty-five.

His father settled against its fabric with a brief smile. Then he looked at his son with concern.

"You told me you were taking the weekend off, but it looks like you just took the work home for the weekend."

Jones leaned back in his chair, officially giving up for the moment.

"I can't help it because it's here," he said, jabbing his finger down on top of one of the loose pieces of paper that had his notes on it. "The answer, the next lead, *something* is here. I know it—I can feel it. I just can't see it. Not yet, at least."

"And you still haven't told anyone at the department what you found out about Annie."

Jones made a half-and-half gesture with his hand.

"Carlos knows I found something new but is giving me some space to pursue it solo. He's taken charge of trying to make sense of Jimmy and all of that that came with him."

His father shook his head.

"I can't imagine why Jimmy said and did what he said and did to you. Do you think he knew you were looking into Annie?"

Carlos had already asked a similar question.

Jones could only shrug.

"I'm not sure how he would've known, but I also don't know why else Jimmy would do that."

His father glanced under the desk at Bonnie. They could only talk about it so much in front of her. Jones didn't want to worry her with their adult problems, after all. His father included.

"Maybe you could use a break then, once your pedicure is finished, of course," he added. "Maybe even invite your new friend over for some lunch?"

Jones knew his father was talking about Cassandra. He also had been told in no uncertain terms that he would love to be the grandfather of their son. Just as he'd shown immediate distaste that Jones wasn't sure what any of their futures looked like yet.

This woman was, after all, someone he'd been thinking about since they'd met seven months ago.

Now that she was within the town limits?

Surely that was the end of that problem, right?

It'd been more than a week since Jones had seen Cassandra and even though he'd spoken his mind to her about their unborn son, he didn't at all feel settled. He wasn't avoiding her, but he also wasn't rushing to try and be at her side.

He just kept thinking about Annie McHale, Lila Shaw and Helen.

Their lives had been taken in one way or another and he'd hadn't done a thing about it.

Not yet, at least.

Lila's tears had been a startling reminder that he could want the world, but wanting wasn't the same as deserving.

Then there was the simple fact that he couldn't protect everyone.

Not when his guard was down.

Not when he was vulnerable.

Not when he was thinking about a future that he'd never once planned on having.

"You talk about someone needing a break? I'd point you right at Cassandra." Jones forced a grin and pushed back in his chair. Bonnie laughed and swatted at his leg.

"Hey! I have the pinky toe to go!"

Jones pointed down at his daughter.

"Cassandra has to deal with little terrors like this every day?" He was all dramatic with his scoff. "I can barely function with this little terror."

Bonnie, having heard the beginning war cry of a play session, scrambled out from under the desk.

"Terror," she yelled. "Terror!"

Jones was up in a flash. He ran around Bonnie until he was out in the hallway. He heard her laugh in delight. She was a girl made for running around.

She was also fast.

They streaked across the one-story house before spilling out into the backyard. Jones might have had much longer legs than his daughter, but Bonnie was lightning-fast. Their chase turned into tag and Bonnie legitimately earned a few of her tags against him.

"When did you get so fast?" he asked after her little hands slapped against his thigh.

Bonnie's cheeks were rosy—her nose, too.

"From the playground," she exclaimed. "I practice there. Practice is how you get good at everything. So I practice and I run and now I'm *super speed*!"

He could tell she was gearing up to run around him again, but she stopped herself and looked down, deeply concerned.

For a brief moment Jones thought something was truly wrong.

But then Bonnie pointed to his foot.

"*Dad.* You smeared your polish!"

Jones laughed as they together surveyed the damage. Running barefoot from the office to outside had upset his glitter-blue toenail polish, leaving some of it on his skin.

"I guess I should've waited for it to dry," he said matter-of-factly. "Then again…"

He hunched over and stuck his hands out to make claws.

"Sometimes you just can't wait to *run fast*!"

Bonnie devolved into giggles as Jones led the charge this time, trying to tag her. He was thankful for his father's large backyard and its lack of prickly weeds, holes and random dog droppings. It made for a more peaceful playtime.

They looped the perimeter without any issues before the back door slid open.

Jones scooped up Bonnie as his latest catch. Her laughter reverberated through him. It hugged into his chest, making all of the uncertainty in life feel less than in an instant.

When he turned to see that his father wasn't watching them alone, he wondered if that warm feeling showed on his face.

"Cassandra," he stated, seeing the woman on the back porch, too. She was smiling.

She was beautiful.

"Miss West!"

Bonnie squirmed out of his hold. She ran full-tilt toward the porch. Her arms were wide open as she collided with Cassandra, who, Jones saw, turned just at the last second to keep her belly from being Bonnie smashed.

"Hey there, Miss Bonnie, how are you doing this lovely Saturday?"

Bonnie, being six, was always one of two things. Talkative and precise with what she said, or talkative and completely random.

She went for random here.

"I had popcorn at school yesterday and Miss Forehand gave us paint for our fingers so we could do some leaves. Mine were really good."

"That's wonderful," Cassandra commented. Jones made his way to their small group.

As soon as he was close enough, Bonnie pointed to his bare feet.

"I painted Dad, too. His toenails. They weren't great before but now they're really pretty. He won't let me do his fingernails because he said it might make everyone else at his work feel left out. I told him that I could come there one day and do everyone's nails, though."

Cassandra nodded and shared the humor in a glance with Jones.

"That would be something I would love to see," she said.

Bonnie was starting to build up to that chaotic energy that small children often got after playing. Jones could sense it and so could his father.

"Hey, Bonbon, I think Ms. West is here to talk to

your dad, so why don't we give them some space and go ahead and make some popcorn here?"

Just like he could sense the chaotic energy, Jones could see that his daughter was conflicted between staying with the new company or eating one of her favorite snacks.

Popcorn won out.

"I can save you some" was all she managed to say to Cassandra as she bounded inside after his father. The little girl could already be heard asking if she could press the buttons on the microwave before the door shut behind them.

Cassandra was still smiling in their direction.

Jones didn't have time to comment before that smile disappeared.

"Did you figure out why Annie McHale kept visiting the study rooms at the library?" Cassandra asked, cutting straight to the point before he could say a word. "Because I think I know how to find out."

CASSANDRA ASKED IF they could continue their conversation on the front porch. She was ready to go, even before she'd stopped by.

She said as much as they backtracked to the porch.

"I'm sorry I showed up, but I was going to call, then realized that we haven't actually exchanged numbers. At least, I don't have yours." She gave him the piece of paper she'd scribbled her number on in the car. "I only know where you live because Millie mentioned your dad's house when we were talking a week or so ago. She's a fan of his flower beds."

Cassandra was vibrating with energy. It was a stark contrast to the exhaustion pregnancy that had been pressing down on her in the last trimester.

So she wanted to go with the flow until that flow stopped.

"I would have just asked for your number from the department, but I didn't want to raise any suspicion."

"Suspicion?" Jones's question had a lot of confusion in it. He'd had his brow scrunched up good since she'd said Annie's name.

"About you doing a second investigation." She dropped her voice a little low despite them being the only people outside that he could see. "I wasn't sure who all knew and if you wanted anyone else to. We end up talking a lot but don't actually answer the important questions around that talking. Like, if I need to ask someone about something that happened on Annie's last day, is it okay for me to come up with a little fib so *they* don't get suspicious?"

Cassandra had been driving herself crazy about this conundrum in the car. It was the only reason she'd come by Jones's house.

At least that's what she was telling herself.

Seeing Jones had been a shock to her system that she hadn't realized she'd needed.

Seeing him playing with his daughter while sporting toenail polish?

Every hormone in her had felt that.

She'd all but needed the walk from the backyard to the front porch to cool herself down and get back on track.

"You shouldn't be doing any investigating." Jones's voice was stern. Authoritative.

Cassandra waved him off.

"It's just me talking with an old friend and then trying to slyly work a question into the conversation. You probably know her. Megan Hamilton. Used to work at the library. Harmless as a container full of Tums. I just don't want to get into any kind of trouble for digging a little if I have to stretch the truth a little."

Jones was shaking his head but not at her concern.

"You aren't in law enforcement, Cassandra. You're not investigating anything. This doesn't concern you."

Cassandra's cheer waned.

Her excitement paused.

She knew she was drawing into herself based solely on the way he was searching her face at the change.

"You didn't see you, Jones. Unconscious behind the wheel of a sinking truck. I did. And I may not have a badge and we might not be a couple, but *you* concern me now." She placed her hand on her stomach. "So I'm going to go ask an old friend a question and if it's worth more than salt, I'm going to call you. It's probably nothing and won't amount to a thing, so don't worry yourself about it, okay? I probably shouldn't have even come by."

She turned on her heel, trying to put a lid on the tangling emotions that were starting to come up more and more frequently around the man.

"Cassandra—" he began.

She didn't turn around but yelled out loud enough so he could hear her.

"Just make sure to keep your phone on, Sheriff."

Chapter Fourteen

Regret.

Fear.

A woman with golden curls and a cot with a plaid blanket.

Cassandra blinked in confusion.

The woman sitting on the bed opposite her was kind enough to explain.

"He didn't hit you, he said, but you have some blood in your hair." Her voice was honey thick with an accent. She touched a spot on her own head. "You were also out like a light when he brought you in. I'm guessing you gave him some trouble and he fought back."

Cassandra was beyond confused, but her first instinct was to touch her stomach. The woman noticed.

"My mama once broke her leg while she was pregnant with my brother. Lost consciousness from the pain for a while. But the doctor said the baby was fine and so was she. It was probably just like you went to sleep. Baby probably doesn't even know otherwise."

Deep and pure fear ran through her, but she finally took in her surroundings.

Which didn't help matters.

"Are we in a motel?"

They were in a room with beige walls, beige carpet, a beige door and beige curtains. The only spots of coloring were on her and the other woman, the flannel blanket and the TV to her left. It was a small flat-screen and had dust covering the screen.

"Looks like it, right? I thought the same." The woman pointed to the nearest window. "I can't tell if we're somewhere high or low. There's no window behind the drapes. That door over there's a bathroom with green tile and that door there—" she pointed to the door across and to the left of Cassandra "—is locked and, I'm thinking, has something mighty heavy against it."

Cassandra didn't know where to go from there.

"I— Why am I here? Who are you?"

"It's the shock. Denial, too, most likely. I had a hard time remembering what happened, too, when I first woke up." The woman sighed. "I know he hit me. I fought him good until it happened."

Cassandra realized she'd been propped up, two pillows behind her. Her memories were fuzzy but starting to come in.

"I was kidnapped by a man." She shook her head, clutching her stomach. "Oh, my God. I was kidnapped."

The woman put her legs over the side of her cot and her back against the wall. She slid up one leg and looped her arms around it.

Resigned—she looked resigned.

"I'm Lottie, Lottie Henderson, and we're in Kelby

Creek as far as I know," she said. "He said you're Cassandra?"

Cassandra nodded. A knot was forming in her throat.

"I knew a Cassie once. Pretty name." The woman let out a breath. "So where did he get you from?"

Cassandra struggled to stand.

She let out a laugh that was close to tears.

"What an awful question," she said.

Lottie wasn't unsympathetic, but she didn't try to apologize for the bluntness. Instead she leaned her head back against the wall.

Cassandra wobbled her way to the door. The lock was on the wrong side. The doorknob didn't budge. She went to the curtains nearest her next.

Lottie was right. There was nothing but smooth wall behind it.

Cassandra's heart plummeted at the sight.

"He said you were a teacher, too," the woman prattled on. "I bet you're good at a lot of things."

"Who has us? How long have you been here?" Cassandra didn't understand why she was getting casual conversation in an absolutely terrifying surrounding.

The woman went on like she hadn't heard her. Cassandra hurried to the other door while she continued. Sure enough it was a small, green-tiled bathroom.

"I've only ever really been good at one thing. Faces. I'm real good at faces. Like, now that I've seen you, I won't forget you. My one dang gift."

Cassandra felt close to tears. She didn't know what to do. Her purse was gone, her phone with it.

She thought of Jones.

She'd called him before she'd seen the man.

He hadn't answered, but surely he'd come for her? Surely, he'd find her?

Cassandra found Lottie's eyes. She was young and beautiful and tired. Her clothes were clean, but she had bruising along the side of her face and a scab over her lip. She had no shoes. Her toenails were painted pink. It was too cheery in contrast.

Cassandra felt her own life fade a little just looking at the woman. She sat back on the cot she'd regained consciousness on and did the only thing she could think of at the moment.

She answered her earlier question.

"New Beginnings Mental Health Facility," Cassandra said. "Well, the old building. The one across the street from the Redman Library."

Lottie snorted, shaking her head as she did so.

"I guess grabbing you wasn't some kind of mistake then."

"What do you mean?"

"My daddy used to work there, at New Beginnings—a name I've found funny since it shut down so quick, by the way—when I was in middle and high school. He did a lot of group therapy there. I used to go there, too, sometimes, since Mama had my brother by accident and I never liked hanging around the house with a toddler." She shrugged. "It wasn't a bad place. Boring since I wasn't let into any of the group meetings and half of that place was closed off to visitors for the more intense cases."

Lottie paused.

Cassandra's adrenaline spiked.

Had she heard something?

Lottie continued after a moment. Cassandra stayed on edge.

"But one day I went to exploring and met a boy in the part of New Beginnings you're not supposed to go. He was nice enough. I thought he was funny. Kept me entertained and feeling all rebellious since no one knew I was hanging around with someone who wasn't even allowed to have shoelaces." She paused again. Cassandra saw now that it was to keep herself collected. "But then one day I went in to see him and he was gone. His things were there but he wasn't. I finally asked my daddy about it and he got so mad. Said he didn't deal with that side of the place. I didn't think anything of it until the Rosewater Inn murder."

Cassandra raised an eyebrow at that. Lottie saw it.

"You're not local, are you?" she asked.

Cassandra shook her head.

"Rosewater Bar used to be the Rosewater Motel, kind of looks like this place if you ask me. Rosewater's had a bunch of owners but the current one finally got some good use out of the building. Split it into three parts. The offices on the left, the bar on the right and the old bed-and-breakfast attempt in the middle. The original owners, though, never wanted all that. They just wanted a motel to make money. Instead they were killed in the lobby one night by some passing guest. At least, that was what everyone thought before they became another cold case in Kelby Creek."

Lottie sighed.

"I didn't think much on it because I was young and self-absorbed, but then on my daddy's last week of work I went back to see if the boy was there," she continued. "He was and he had a look about him that was different. Then he asked me about the killings and I just couldn't get over how he looked when he did that. I swear, every part of me stood on end. It was like he was bragging about something he didn't do. But then, I realized he'd been missing the same time as the owners were killed."

She shook her head.

"I told my daddy about it, he told his boss and I didn't go back. Which worked out since Daddy started working at the hospital after that. But nothing happened and I got older and forgot about it. Met a man who drives me crazy and decided it was time I tried to show him how much I did love him."

Lottie had tears in her eyes now.

"There's a clearing in the Kintucket Woods that looks just about heaven on a clear night. Stars as far as you can dream 'em. I wanted to surprise him with a little camping trip, so I went on out to the hardware store in town to get a tent. That's where I saw a man and, even though he'd aged, I hadn't forgotten his face."

"The boy at New Beginnings." Cassandra wanted to be clear.

Lottie nodded.

"I guess he hadn't forgotten mine," she said. "He surprised me at the woods when I was setting up. Must've followed me. I've been here ever since."

"Who is he?" Cassandra asked. "What's his name? And *why* are we here?"

Lottie pulled up her other leg and turned her body until she was lying down across her cot. She answered but she kept her eyes up at the ceiling.

"Killian Carmichael," she said. "He's tall, slender. Has light brown hair. Pale, too. He's given me food, clean clothes and hasn't touched me since he brought me here. I think he's really smart, too. I think he has some kind of plan, but I don't know what it is. If he got you because you were poking around New Beginnings, then I'm thinking you ruffled his feathers somehow. Maybe he likes his privacy."

"I wasn't there for him." Cassandra had been there for Annie McHale. For what she'd found out at Megan Hamilton's house.

Lottie shrugged. The movement made her cot squeak.

"Whatever you did, you got in his way."

Cassandra had no idea.

She'd never heard of the name Killian Carmichael.

She didn't know what he could possibly want with her.

A pop of pressure went against the palm she had over her stomach.

Cassandra could have cried.

It was a kick.

Relief washed over her.

Just as fast as despair.

She should have listened to Jones. She should have never tried to play detective.

Now she only hoped he could follow her misguided path to save her and their child before it was too late.

JONES HAD EVERY intention of following Cassandra after she left, but like when they first met, their timing was off.

Jones had gone back inside for his rental car keys and run smack-dab into a problem. His dad had his phone out to him.

"Carlos called, then Foster, then Brutus. Followed by Carlos again."

"I've only been outside a minute," Jones said. "What has everyone calling?"

His dad didn't know but they both found out soon enough.

Carlos was nearly breathless when he answered Jones's return call. He got straight to the point.

"Jimmy and Nan just told the press that you're re-investigating the Annie McHale kidnapping case. And, Jones, everyone is losing their minds over it."

Jones had started looking for his shoes.

"We knew this would happen eventually," he told his chief deputy. "I'm not ashamed of what I'm doing. It's no secret."

"I agree with all of that," Carlos said. "But, Sheriff, the news is running through town like wildfire and a lot of people are having some feelings about it. We might need you at the department sooner rather than later."

Jones had meant what he said—he wasn't trying to

keep the investigation a secret. He *was* trying to keep it on the down-low until he knew more.

"I'm on my way," he said, finding his socks and slipping them over his glitter-covered toenails. "Don't say a word to anyone until I'm in."

After that Jones became the sheriff he didn't like. The PR sheriff. The one who talked to the press and said vague things and sidestepped any information that would hurt an ongoing investigation. He talked to the local news anchor only and said he was looking into a lot of older cases. Annie's was among them.

That was it.

That was enough.

The next two hours were a swamp mess of phone calls, drop-bys and social-media-comment wars.

It wasn't until he found the space to breathe by himself that he realized his dad's old phone had a piss-poor ringer.

He'd missed a call.

From Cassandra.

Guilt struck him like lightning.

He should have called her after the news broke.

He hoped Megan Hamilton hadn't given her too hard of a time if they'd found out together she might be looking into Annie, too.

The phone call had been left an hour before.

There was a voice mail.

"Hey, Jones, it's Cassandra. I just finished with Megan and I think Annie wasn't actually interested in the library at all." Jones could hear a car door shut.

"I think she was sneaking out across the street. I'm—I'm there now and going to give a quick peek around. It's—it's okay. Wow I'm out of breath. Ha, ha. It's this pregnancy stuff. I used to be in shape. Anyway, I'm here and just going to look around. It's not like anyone is going to stop me. This place has been closed a while. All right, long rambling message over. I'll call you after just so you know my super sleuthing hasn't gotten me into trouble."

The recording ended.

Jones looked at the time stamp again.

There were no new calls.

He pressed the call-back option.

It rang and rang and rang.

Cassandra didn't answer.

Jones hung up.

Then he tried again.

No Cassandra.

Jones stood. He replayed her message as he pulled his coat off the back of his office chair.

"You don't say where you are, Cassandra," he said, griping at the phone.

No, she had told him. Across the street from the library. That's what she said.

Jones took a second, but he figured it out.

New Beginnings, the mental health and rehabilitation center.

But it was closed, like she said.

Why was she there?

And why wasn't she answering her phone?

Jones had his keys and was out of the department in a flash.

He decided right then and there he wasn't letting Cassandra out of his sight from now on.

Not until they figured out what was going on in Kelby Creek.

Chapter Fifteen

New Beginnings had once been housed in an expansive building. Some parts had two stories, the back half had a still-impressive fence despite being abandoned, and even with some of the doors and windows boarded up, it was in relatively good shape.

Jones got out of his car and experienced an awful sense of déjà vu.

Cassandra's car was in the side parking lot, but she wasn't in it.

Jones tried to call her again.

No luck.

He took a second to look toward the library. A lead he'd been obsessing about meant nothing to him now.

"Do you think she went inside?"

Carlos was with him. Jones hadn't wanted to take any chances. If Cassandra had found trouble, he wasn't going to lone-wolf it if he didn't have to.

"She said she was going to poke around." Jones tapped his service weapon in its holster twice and headed for the sidewalk. "Since she's not answering her phone, I'm really hoping she *is* in there sleuthing around."

Carlos fell into step behind him, the chief deputy also on high alert.

On the car ride over, Jones had caught him up on everything Cassandra and he had found out in the last two weeks. He'd been impressed by Cassandra's go-get-'em attitude. Jones had shaken his head, angry with himself that he'd let her go out alone.

The side door was locked tight. Carlos spread out across the windows trying to see if they had a line of sight inside.

They didn't.

Jones led them to the front doors to the same setup—locked.

Carlos knocked.

There was no movement inside as far as they could tell.

The back of the building had more potential access points, but all were boarded or locked up.

"Let me call again," Jones said, feeling as tense as could be.

Where was she?

Why was her car in the lot?

Carlos walked to the back door that fed directly into the staff parking lot.

"I never understood why this place didn't sell," he said, more to himself than to Jones. "It's not like anyone is using—"

Carlos stopped talking.

Jones moved the phone down to his side.

A ringtone was going off inside.

It timed perfectly with the ringing phone in his hand.

Carlos shared a look with Jones, but he was already moving.

With a kick that had no forethought, just anxious power, Jones broke the wooden door like it was nothing more than a toothpick.

"Cassandra?"

His voice echoed out.

Nothing but a ringing phone came back.

LOTTIE WAS QUIET for a while.

Cassandra couldn't handle it.

"Listen, there's a man out there I have to apologize to, a kid in here that I have to watch grow up, and I can't do either one if this Killian guy decides to really hurt me." Cassandra was up on her feet, pacing. "I get not being able to escape earlier when it was just you, Lottie, but now you're not alone. I'm here and I'm going to need us to be somewhere other than here real quick."

Lottie, who'd been weepy on and off after her story before going stone-cold quiet, stirred a little.

"No offense, but he's a big guy and you're pregnant. What if he has a gun? A knife? Any kind of weapon?"

Cassandra had already thought about that.

When she'd first seen him outside of New Beginnings, his hands had been free. When he approached her, she didn't remember seeing anything that was a weapon, either.

"When he comes in for you, does he ever have a gun or knife or anything?"

Lottie sat up.

"He had a Taser once, a baseball bat another time. Once he said if I got past him I'd regret it quick. The last time he came in, before you, I got a hit in and he got…well, this."

She motioned to her bruising along her face.

Cassandra winced.

Then she tried to rally.

"Me and my kids got trapped in a storage room at my school last week and how I got us out was by bum-rushing the man as soon as he opened the door. Just literally running at him. Maybe we could do something like that? Catch him by surprise?"

Lottie clearly didn't like the plan.

It wasn't like Cassandra did, either.

"We could be killed in this room for trying and no one would ever know."

"Who's to say that isn't already the plan?"

Cassandra felt sick for saying it.

She knew Lottie knew it was true, though.

She nodded.

"Okay, then but let's try to be smart about this."

There wasn't much smarts to be had about rushing at a kidnapper, but they tried their best. Cassandra went to the bathroom and managed to get the towel rack free from the wall. It was old, cheap plastic, but it could do something. She looked wistfully at where the mirror should have been. Shards of glass wrapped in the linens.

It was a movie-magic move that she'd seen a few times.

It would have been nice to have the option now.

"Maybe we can do something with the cots," Lottie mused out loud when Cassandra deemed the rest of the bathroom's contents unusable. "Maybe flip one up and use it like a battering ram? I think it would fit through the door okay. Push him down at least."

"That could work! We can ram him and then hit him with everything we have. Literally everything we have." She pointed to the standing lamp between the cots. Then the TV.

It was a wild plan, one built on absolute desperation, but Cassandra felt a flair of hope at it.

A flair that fizzled when the sound of a door unlocking filled the room.

"He doesn't come until night," Lottie whispered, panicked. "He's early."

Cassandra didn't have time to rally again. She moved to her cot and was glad Lottie went with her. They had it hoisted up between them and were turning toward the door, not at all ready to take on Killian when he came through.

But the door didn't open.

They took a few steps closer, listening.

Footsteps, clear as day.

Yet, they were retreating.

Cassandra shared a look with Lottie.

"Is this a trick?" the woman whispered.

Cassandra didn't know but she wasn't going to let an unlocked door go unopened for long.

"Come on."

They put down the cot and collected their individual makeshift weapons. Cassandra had the plastic towel rack, Lottie picked up the lamp. Unplugging it caused the room to be dotted in darkness. Cassandra hadn't been there long, but she knew she would have nightmares about it and its beige awfulness.

She motioned for Lottie to stand to the side and tried the doorknob.

It was smooth as it turned.

Adrenaline rushed through her. Cassandra took a breath and nodded at Lottie.

She opened the door slowly, then stopped, waiting for resistance from their kidnapper.

There was none.

There was no one and nothing on the other side of the door.

Cassandra tapped Lottie's shoulder.

She waved her to follow.

The room opened up into a small hallway that led to a landing that made no sense to Cassandra. To the left and right there was only enough space to walk a few steps to each side. The walls matched the floor—both were concrete. An electrical box was on the left wall, a metal box sat on the floor to the right.

Straight ahead were steep, metal stairs.

Cassandra only cared about them.

Lottie stopped her before she could step on the first one. She pointed to Cassandra's belly and pushed in front of her, taking the lead.

Cassandra let her but she tightened her hold on the towel rod as she followed up.

The stairs squealed under their weight. Cassandra winced at each step. The door at the top of the stairs matched the metal. It, however, didn't make a sound when Lottie opened it.

Cold air pushed into them the second it was open.

If Cassandra hadn't equated moving forward to survival, she might have stopped to question what it was she was seeing with more attention.

They'd gone from a motel-looking room with carpet and a bathroom, to concrete and metal, to…a dirt floor and wood walls and a ceiling that had seen better days.

Lottie must have been on the same wavelength. She looked around but never slowed down.

Not until they got to another door.

It was wooden, too, but looked new.

She waited until Cassandra gave her the nod to go ahead before opening it.

The cold that pressed against them was several degrees lower. Lottie put her hands over her eyes in what must have been reflex. She hadn't seen the sun in a week.

"Where are we?" Cassandra breathed out, as she peered out at a stand of trees.

Trees stretched all through Kelby Creek and beyond, the heaviest area at the Kintucket Woods near the town limits. At least that's what June had told her when a field-trip idea to go on a nature hike through them had been suggested.

Cassandra wasn't local, though.

To her she was looking at a foreboding forest, one cutting her off from safety.

She turned around to where they'd come from.

It looked like a utility shed or small barn from their new vantage point.

That made the imagery and its placement all the more menacing.

"Let's go," Cassandra said. She took Lottie's free hand and pulled her along into the closest tree line. There was a small path, but she wasn't going to walk right into Killian returning.

Or whoever had unlocked the door and then promptly left.

Lottie didn't argue with the plan of fleeing into the woods, even as her feet started to bleed the more they went.

Cassandra wanted to mull over their situation, trying to put two and two together, from her looking into Annie McHale at New Beginnings, but the longer they went, the more her mind only settled on one thing.

Jones.

He had to find them.

He was local.

He was the sheriff.

Surely, he could figure out what happened?

And if he didn't?

Cassandra stopped her train of thought there before looping back and replaying it again.

It wasn't until Lottie slowed that Cassandra realized she wasn't just thinking of Jones in desperation.

Thinking of him was bringing her comfort.

She trusted him without knowing him all that well. She just *did*.

And that wasn't some small thing.

"There's something—something up ahead." Lottie's voice came out, panting.

Cassandra wasn't far behind. She'd been winded for the last mile or so, she guessed.

If they didn't find something soon, she was going to have to stop and rest.

Lottie pointed out in front of them and a little to the right.

"I see it!"

The woods ended a few feet from them and Lottie was right. There was something in the distance beyond that.

A house.

A big house.

Cassandra started forward, thankful all the way to the tips of her toes that they would be getting out of the woods, but Lottie stopped her dead in her tracks.

Her face had contorted into a mixture of what seemed to be confusion and fear.

"What is it?"

Lottie shook her head.

"I know where we are and—and we don't need to go there." She pointed to their left. "There's a—there's a road we can walk along for a little bit. More houses."

Cassandra didn't understand.

"Where are we?"

Lottie started to walk along the tree line, giving the house in the distance a wide berth that was worrisome.

"That's the McHale Manor."

Cassandra didn't move to follow.

"The McHale Manor? Annie McHale's home?"

Lottie didn't break stride.

"Yep. Right before she disappeared forever. I don't know about you but I don't want to disappear forever too. Let's—"

"Cassandra!"

Lottie stopped dead in her tracks. Cassandra froze too.

"Cassandra!"

The call came again. It was far off.

It was near the house.

Lottie's eyes were wide, terrified.

Cassandra was thawing.

"I know that voice," she whispered, as if saying it any louder would somehow make it less true.

She waited for one more call.

It came.

"Cassandra!"

She didn't need any more confirmation.

Cassandra took a step forward and yelled out for all she was worth.

"Jones!"

It was like her voice had a line tethered to the man. She and Lottie watched as the towering sheriff came running around the house in the distance. It was too far away to see his exact expression, but Cassandra knew he was searching for her.

Cassandra ran out of the tree line but stopped before she was in the open clearing between the woods and the house.

"Jones," she yelled again.

The sheriff's head turned. He saw her and he was running.

Cassandra wanted to say a lot of things—warn him of Killian, whoever freed them, explain Lottie and say how she knew he'd come—but the second Jones was close enough to touch, she crumpled.

"I'm sorry," she cried out before he could touch her. "I'm so sorry."

Jones had never slowed on approach. He collided into her with warmth and care of her stomach.

She accepted the strength of his arms as they wrapped around her.

"You're safe now," he said into her hair. "I got you."

Cassandra didn't think their troubles were over yet, but in that moment, she found she didn't care.

Chapter Sixteen

Ray Cooke came into the hospital lobby like a bat outta hell. His eyes were red. He was upset.

And Jones knew half of it was at himself.

"Ray," Jones called, waving him over. Jones knew he was coming and had been waiting by the first set of elevators.

Ray ran to him, not wasting a second.

Jones figured he'd do the same so he hit the button to call the elevator down before the man had made it to him.

"She's okay, right? You said she was okay?" Any animosity Ray had been harboring almost two weeks ago, when Jones had found him drunk on the bridge, was long gone. He was a man worried and sick with guilt at the same time.

"Lottie's good," Jones confirmed. "She's got some bruises and her feet are a bit scraped up but she's still as good as she was when I called."

The elevator doors opened. Ray only seemed partially relieved. He stepped inside after Jones shook his head.

"I—I was sure she'd left me again. You know? She

was gone, the car was gone. I—I didn't know she'd been—"

The doors shut in time for Ray to make a noise somewhere between a yell and a groan.

Jones felt for the man.

After he'd found out that Lottie had been held captive for a week with no one knowing, he'd gone through a volley of emotions as sheriff. As someone meant to stop this sort of thing from happening.

He couldn't imagine how Ray felt knowing he'd not been looking for Lottie the whole time she was gone.

Cassandra had been missing for almost two hours and it had been eating Jones alive every second.

"The important thing is that she's okay. She's safe now. And the first person she asked after was you. She's not upset, Ray. She's just tired, scared and wants nothing and no one but you to be by her side."

Jones wasn't exaggerating or fibbing to make the man feel better. The first thing Lottie had said in the car on the ride to the hospital was that she wanted Ray.

Cassandra had held her hand in the back seat and promised her they'd get him.

Jones would never forget how calm her voice was then, how reassuring.

How tired and drained it was at the same time.

Tears streaked down her face, and there was blood in her hair.

Even now Jones wanted to punch something to get his anger out.

Instead he took a breath.

The doors to the third floor opened. A deputy from the department nodded to Jones.

"Now, Ray, you're one of three visitors allowed on this floor at the moment," Jones told him, turning the man in the right direction. "I don't know Lottie's family-and-friend situation, but we'd like to keep it to you for now."

Ray nodded. His anger and guilt had turned to an anxiousness that was rubbing off on Jones. He didn't even ask any follow-up questions.

Jones didn't blame him.

He showed him to the door of Lottie's hospital room.

Ray knocked once then disappeared in a rush inside.

Before the door closed behind him, Jones heard Lottie cry out. Ray was blubbering in an instant.

It made Jones soften.

The door across the hall was already cracked open. Jones went inside and walked into a conversation with Cassandra and Carlos.

Seeing her sitting in a hospital bed made his blood boil.

She shouldn't have been there at all.

"Ask her already," she said to Carlos. When she saw Jones, she went from smiling to concerned. "Did you get Ray to Lottie?"

Jones nodded.

"I think that's the first time I've spent with Ray without threatening jail time." He took a seat on the chair next to the bed. It had become his designated spot since they'd brought the women in. "I gotta say, it was nice."

"I just hope that will give Lottie some good to go

on." Cassandra shook her head. "I was in that bunker for way less than a day and I don't think I can ever go into a windowless room again. I can't imagine being down there for over a week."

The three of them were quiet a moment at that admission.

Whatever Carlos and she had been discussing beforehand fell by the wayside. Carlos cleared his throat.

"I'm headed back to the McHale house to talk with Foster and Kenneth," he told Jones. "Then I'm back at the department. Cole is taking night shift."

Jones nodded. In between trying to figure out what was going on, they'd had to deal with their schedules.

Especially since Jones had changed his around, something that he hadn't yet had the chance to tell Cassandra about.

Then again, they hadn't been alone together since he'd embraced her out behind the McHale house.

Carlos dipped his head to Cassandra, said he was glad she was feeling good and then headed out.

Jones caught himself looking at Cassandra's belly before *she* caught him looking, too.

"The doctor gave us the all clear," she reminded him. "Baby boy and me. Strong heartbeat for him, no concussion for me. We're good."

Jones growled a little.

"You shouldn't be in this place at all."

It was a comment he'd doled out several times already. This time, though, Cassandra smiled.

"Well, I'm going to count it as an impromptu practice run for when I most definitely *have* to be here in a few months. At least now I'm not in any pain."

Jones did his best job at giving a smile to her attempt to lighten the mood. She must have realized it hadn't budged him much.

"I shouldn't have played detective, I'm sorry," she said. "I just wanted to help and I thought I could do that without getting in anyone's way. Honestly, had I known what would happen I never would have risked it. Risked us."

Her hand smoothed over her belly.

It did something to him. Jones tried to let go of some of his tension.

"You don't have to keep apologizing, Cassandra. I'm the one who didn't go with you. This is on me."

She reached out and took his hand in one fluid movement. He was glad there were no IVs in it. The sight would have brought out his rage at whoever had done this to her again.

"Unless you managed to attack and kidnap me during a press conference, I'm not blaming you at all. Especially since you're the one who found us after the fact."

Jones could have taken the comment with grace. Then simmered down because his heightened stress wasn't helping anyone.

But they hadn't been alone yet. He hadn't had the chance to tell her what had really happened.

Why he had been at the McHale house in the first place.

Cassandra let go of his hand, an eyebrow raising in the process.

"What?" she asked.

Jones used to think he was a closed book. That wasn't the case with her.

He had a few more specific questions for her before he dove into his answer.

"You said you went to the library study room and found nothing, just like I did when I went, but noticed the window in one showed New Beginnings across the road. What made you go to Megan Hamilton about it?"

"I noticed Lloyd was still using paper logs for reservations and, since Megan used to work there before him, I wanted to know where older logs might be. I taught Megan's granddaughter two years ago and became friends with Megan so she had no problem when I asked about it. Or, at least she didn't pick apart my lame explanation for looking for a former student's older sister. I phrased it to kind of sound like the student had been adopted and I was trying to find her family on the down-low." Cassandra squirmed a little. "I'm not proud of being dishonest, but, well, it worked out alright."

She motioned to her phone on the table next to him.

"Megan had some of the old logs stashed in her attic. She was told she could take them when she retired and use them to make her flowers."

Jones gave her a look.

"She makes and sells paper flowers on Etsy," she explained. "Her house is filled with them."

Jones lifted her phone and handed it over.

"*But* she hadn't gotten to using them yet since her neighbor gave her crates of old newspapers, so I was able to look at the logs myself." She clicked through her phone until she got to a picture. She handed it back to him. "Annie's name wasn't on any of the old ones, the ones before she was kidnapped, but Jasmine Lohan's name appears on the reservation log every Saturday, Monday and Thursday morning for at least two months and only for the room with the window. I asked Megan if she remembered Jasmine, noting that the name appeared a lot, and she actually laughed. *She said* that half of the time Jasmine would slip in and out without her even noticing. That it happened so much the staff started calling her the Ghost in the Stacks." Cassandra was clearly amused by the name, but that feeling went away at the next part.

"Then Megan said Annie McHale went missing and the whole town kind of stopped. Jasmine stopped reserving the room and, at least while Megan was on schedule, didn't come back to the library again."

Jones looked down at the picture on Cassandra's phone.

"This is one of the old logs?"

She nodded.

"So it sounds like Annie wasn't the one reserving the study room, it was Jasmine."

"Or Annie reserving under Jasmine's name. Ghost in the Stacks sounds like someone who doesn't really want to be seen."

Jones conceded that.

"That got me wondering about the why of it all and I started thinking about that window and New Beginnings and looked it up." Cassandra started talking with her hands, excited as she continued. "Did you know that New Beginnings was partially funded by the Delphi Group? And, did you know that the Delphi Group is an offshoot of the McHale Foundation?"

Jones did know about the Delphi Group but he hadn't known that it was a part of the McHale charity organization.

Jones cracked a quick grin.

"Remind me after the baby is born to see if you want to switch jobs to detective."

"I don't think it's some big, dark secret or anything, but I don't think a lot of people know that," she said. "It got me a lot more curious about New Beginnings, though. If Annie was reserving the room with the window that faced New Beginnings, a place her parents helped create, then maybe she was going across the street during her reservation times."

"Why go through the trouble of going to the library at all if you're just going to use someone else's name and not stay?" Jones added.

At that, Cassandra shrugged.

"Maybe in case she got caught she wanted an alibi? One where she could get Jasmine to admit that it was Annie reserving the room so Annie could get some privacy? I don't know but that's a good question. I would be more inclined to think the whole idea of her going to New Beginnings was ridiculous had I not gone there myself and, well—"

"—been taken," he said, finishing the thought.

Cassandra nodded.

"Then there's the whole secret room thing I woke up in that just so happened to be on the McHale property.

I thought I was somewhere in that New Beginnings place. If that's all unrelated then you can slap my butt and call me Sally."

Jones chuckled at the phrase.

Then he sighed.

"It's definitely related." It was his turn to pull out his phone. He went to the gallery app. "I didn't just guess that you were at the McHale house. *This* was left next to your phone inside of New Beginnings."

He clicked the picture he was looking for and handed it over. The picture on the screen was burned into his mind.

A single piece of paper with one line perfectly written on it.

"'She's at the house—Annie.'"

Cassandra read the message, twice.

It gave him chills both times.

"Wait. Annie? Annie McHale?"

Jones shrugged.

"We don't know who Killian is yet, or why he's doing what he's doing, but this could be his way of being dramatic," he offered. "Or trying to distract us. I wouldn't read too much in to it yet. Not until we know more."

Cassandra didn't respond right away. Her eyes were scanning the message again.

Jones watched her.

He marveled at how much she'd grown to care about Annie's case, his case, since finding out about it.

Then again, Jones had a sneaking suspicion that that's just what Cassandra did.

She cared.

But even those who cared got frustrated enough from time to time.

"Ugh. This is all giving me a headache." She handed him his phone back. "Every time I talk to you I feel like I have more questions than there can possibly be answers to."

"I can say ditto to that."

Cassandra let out a breath that sunk her low.

She was tired.

He didn't blame her.

"The doc said we can leave when you're ready. Then we can run by your place and grab your things. Carlos already had someone get your car from New Beginnings."

"Why are we grabbing my things?"

Her confusion was genuine.

It made Jones smirk, despite how serious he was when he answered.

"Because, Miss West, you're staying with me tonight."

Chapter Seventeen

Bonnie was over the moon about the company. She yelled Cassandra's name like she was some kind of movie star and Bonnie was her biggest fan.

"You've made quite the impression on our girl," Jones's father, Ted, said when Bonnie ran off to get her favorite toys to show her.

Cassandra had felt a blush rise at that comment. There was just something special about being accepted by kids. Even more so by being accepted by Jones's daughter.

"I'd have to say likewise to that," she told him. Ted smiled. He'd been doing it off and on between the several times he'd asked how she was feeling since she and Jones had arrived at the house earlier.

She'd told him, at every turn, that she was fine.

She was, after all

Her baby had gotten the all clear and she would sleep better knowing that Lottie was safe at the hospital under guard. Not to mention half of the Dawn County Sheriff's Department now were looking into the bunker, New Beginnings and the man named Killian Carmichael.

As far as Jones said, after the update he received when dinner was wrapping up, Killian was still their biggest mystery. There were no records of him at New Beginnings or in their system, and no one recognized the name. Ted had even pulled security-camera footage from the hardware store after Lottie's statement that she'd seen Killian outside of it before he'd followed her to the clearing.

All customers seen on the camera were regulars and well-known. Still, Lottie looked at pictures of each when they'd been brought to her in the hospital. She recognized none.

"A sketch artist should be here in the morning. Hopefully with the description Lottie gives we can find this Killian guy."

Jones concluded his conversation with Carlos and dropped down onto the couch. Cassandra and Ted had been talking about the upcoming school schedule and field trips. She'd caught him looking at her belly several times.

Once again, she realized that with all the talking that she and Jones had done at the hospital, they hadn't broached the subject of who knew the identity of her child's father.

It didn't feel right to potentially be the first to tell Ted. That was Jones's decision to make, she decided.

"So what happens now?" Cassandra asked when Jones closed his eyes to rest for a moment. "Surely you're not going back to the department. You're clearly exhausted, too."

Jones shook his head.

"I'm not going back to the department until we've gotten some more answers."

Cassandra hadn't expected that response.

"He took himself off schedule for the next few days," Ted said. "He wanted to make sure we were all safe. We also have a cruiser outside. I think it's Sterling, if I'm not mistaken."

"It is. He insisted. Marigold, too." Jones opened his eyes. They were red.

When was the last time he'd gotten good sleep?

Cassandra focused on the significant part a second later.

Jones had stepped aside to keep them safe. Keep all of them safe.

It warmed her.

Him demanding she stay by his side?

That had done a bit more.

She hadn't known she could get butterflies while carrying a baby.

But she had.

She got them again now.

"Both are good eggs," Ted continued. "I'll get them some food in the morning. I know Sterling's a fan of my coffee."

He rocked up out of his chair. He was wearing cargo shorts and the two scars around his knee were shining and wide.

He noticed her stare and smiled.

"Us Murphys are a strong breed. Every single one of us."

Ted winked and then said good-night. His room was on the far side of the house. Jones didn't speak until they heard the door close.

"He knows about the baby." Jones gave a soft chuckle. "Heck, he even knew about us meeting all those months ago. I'm actually impressed he didn't outright blurt it at you when you first came in."

That blush came back quickly.

"I thought he might. The whole Murphy-strong-breed comment and all."

Jones snorted this time. He didn't follow it up with a comment on his father, though. He nodded to the hallway across from them.

"Dad gave me the master bedroom when I moved in since it's got this weird step-down situation and the bathroom isn't as crutch-and-wheelchair friendly. I got him to set it up for you when we were at your place earlier."

Jones stood up and reached a hand down to her. She was thankful for the assist. Her belly wasn't exactly beach-ball-size, but she was finding it harder and harder to stand up from anything with comfortable cushions.

"Bonnie is on the other side of the house and a hard sleeper, so if you need to get up and go to the kitchen or just move around, don't worry about waking her," he continued. They'd made it to the door. He opened it and waved her in. "There's new sheets on the bed and clean towels and whatnot in the bathroom. I also made some space in the dresser for you, top drawer."

"You didn't have to do all of this," she said honestly.

Jones waved her off.

"Least I could do. You did, after all, jump into a creek to save me."

His smile was teasing.

Cassandra couldn't help her third blush of the night.

She went to her bags on the bed to create distance from him and those dang butterflies that started flapping.

Jones had already made his position on them together clear and she respected that.

In fact, she agreed with it.

Being co-parents might be difficult, but it wouldn't be heartbreaking.

Not like what they had both already experienced.

If she could avoid that again?

Then she could handle swatting away butterflies every now and then.

"All right, well, I think you're just about right on the dot with the whole rest thing." He grabbed a pillow and blanket that was sitting on top of the dresser. "I'll be out on the couch if you need me."

"The couch?" Cassandra hadn't thought about his sleeping arrangements yet. "Oh, that isn't fair, Jones. Take the bed and I'll take the couch."

The man shook his head.

"Good night, Cassandra."

"Jones, really I don't mind if you—"

"Good night," he repeated. The door shut between them.

Cassandra stared at it a moment.

"Good night, Jones."

THE HOUSE WAS QUIET.

Though, since Bonnie had come into his life, quiet didn't really mean the same thing.

Jones stood in the doorway of her bedroom. Her sound machine's white noise was whirling by the window. Her stars of blue and green light swam across the ceiling. Bonnie was breathing deep and steady.

Jones took his pillow and blanket and laid on the carpet next to her bed.

The Almost Pink paint still seemed bright in the dark.

Jones wished Helen was here, wished she could see the paint. Wished she could see Bonnie sleeping, and laughing, and living wild.

He wished he could tell her that Bonnie, despite all of his failures as a father so far, was kind and smart and filled with more courage than he thought was possible for her small size. That she was loved deeply by his father and, although they hadn't been close, Helen's parents came to visit them always for Christmas.

He wished he could tell her he was afraid that one day Bonnie would blame him for everything that had happened to Kelby Creek. To her. To their family.

That one day she'd be old enough to understand that a lot of people in this world were broken by one thing or another. That life could be mean for no good reason.

That some things just couldn't be fixed.

Jones also wished he could tell Helen about Cassandra, as odd as it might have sounded.

About his fear of being a father again, to a boy, at that.

And, even though he spent his time behind a badge, his courage about the future had been crippled by her death.

When the sun goes away, you just don't look at light the same way anymore.

Jones listened to Bonnie breathing, unaware of him on her floor, wishing he could talk to her mama.

Unaware that his heart was stretching across the house to a woman who had shown nothing but kindness and patience to her.

Jones tried to sleep, he really did, but the usual quietness of the house had him tossing and turning.

He didn't know why until he was standing in front of his bedroom door.

The soft light of the bedside lamp reached out beneath it. Jones almost turned around. Then he heard the sound of a phone being laid down on the nightstand. The same sound he heard overnight when he plugged his phone into the charger.

He knocked lightly.

Cassandra called out, just as quietly.

Jones let himself in and shut the door back behind him.

Cassandra was propped up with two pillows, her body covered by his sheets. She gave him a look of such acute concern, he hesitated.

"Is everything okay?" she asked, trying to sit up straighter.

Jones had every intention of saying he just had come in to check on her. That he was anxious given the last two weeks, especially that day.

But he didn't come close to his intention.

Jones went to the side of the bed. He placed one hand on the headboard over her and the other under her chin. She watched him, bright eyes wide, as he bent low.

Jones pressed his lips to hers.

It was a slow kiss. It was a soft kiss.

It was his way of opening up.

Of saying he was sorry.

Of saying he was glad she was okay.

That she was there with him, with his family, all okay.

That he was sorry he couldn't say all of that out loud.

That the kiss was all he could give her now.

So he made it last.

Cassandra returned it, her hands coming up to either side of his face.

For the first time in a long while, Jones felt content.

He knew it couldn't last.

He ended the kiss and met her gaze, still cradled in her hands.

He didn't know what to say.

She did.

"Stay with me tonight. I don't want to be alone."

Her voice was soft.

Jones nodded.

Cassandra let him go. He went to the other side of the bed and took off his shirt. The sheets were cool against his skin as he slid between them.

Cassandra kept quiet while he molded around her body, arm around her, leg between hers. She reached over to turn off the light.

Darkness filled the room.

Jones let Cassandra adjust beneath him. When she settled he put his chin on top of her shoulder.

He remembered the first night they'd lain together.

The lead-up to it had been a quiet kind of chaos.

They'd eaten at a restaurant but hadn't wanted to part ways yet. So they'd gone to a coffee shop. It had closed right as they'd hit the door. They'd then found themselves walking around the hotel before taking a stroll by the pool. There, their conversation had turned into something more.

When she'd invited him in after her, when he'd walked her to her room, Jones knew what saying yes would become.

He'd kissed her deep and true two steps inside. His hands had caressed her cheek before he'd used them to take her to the bed. She was nothing to his size, like moving air.

She had laughed at the quick move.

He had kissed that laughter.

Then he'd kissed all of her.

After that they'd been a tangle of skin, warmth and the best kind of movement.

The morning after, she'd smiled up at him. Quiet, bright. The sunlight that had managed to find the only crack between the curtains, lying across her shoulder— the same shoulder he was pressed against now—and Jones had suspected something then, right then.

Despite not really knowing her, he was never going to forget her.

Jones moved his hand over her stomach in the dark. She covered it with her own.

A few minutes later and Jones was fast asleep.

Chapter Eighteen

There were three doughnuts in a bag sitting next to the bed when Cassandra awoke the next morning.

One was chocolate, one was powdered sugar and one had a bite taken out of it. A little perfect Bonnie-size bite, if she had to guess.

Cassandra ran her hand over the empty spot next to her in bed after making the discovery.

Last night had been…different.

That kiss?

Every butterfly Cassandra had been swatting away had come back in full force. They'd brought their friends and families and even coworkers to the party.

It had been all Cassandra could do to not completely melt into it.

Into him.

But then she'd seen it in his eyes.

Jones Murphy had been feeling something and that something wasn't up to her to define. So she'd let him take the lead.

That had led to a giant of a man wrapping around her in the darkness.

Cassandra had felt him relax against her and then, sure enough, his breathing had evened out.

She'd fallen asleep a little later.

She was a little let down that she hadn't felt him leave when he'd woken.

Cassandra stretched wide and tried to stay in her happy bubble for the moment. She found her phone and unlocked it. It was nine on Sunday. Which meant, for once, she'd slept through the night without having to readjust or use the bathroom. It was a small blessing.

Now that blessing had run its course. She went to the bathroom, decided to go ahead and shower and found herself back in the bedroom getting dressed while eating a doughnut.

She dipped into her purse for her prenatal vitamins and looked at the bed.

Then she was thinking about the cot in the bunker on the McHale property. They'd been told the day before that it was a storm shelter for tornadoes. One that had been installed by Annie's grandparents and then shuttered and locked down after Annie was taken and her parents moved.

They'd had no idea that someone was using it.

Why would they?

They were living in Montana now.

Cassandra ran a hand over her stomach. Her heart hurt just thinking about the possibility of her son being taken.

Gone for years with no answers.

So depressed and heartbroken that she'd have to escape the town they'd spent their life in.

But Cassandra wouldn't leave, no matter how much it hurt.

She'd have to stay, go through every tree in the woods and turn over every pebble by the creek.

Jones would do the same, she was sure of it. He might have left Kelby Creek behind after his wife was killed—hadn't Cassandra left her previous life after Ryan had passed?—but she had no doubt that he'd stay if Bonnie was gone without a trace. That thought led Cassandra down a rabbit hole of what-ifs and more questions.

She knew she could get lost there, but now wasn't the time.

They didn't need her help to solve their mysteries. She'd already overstepped once and look where that had landed her.

Cassandra thought about that cot again, and pictured Lottie's bruises along her face. She thought about the man who'd taken her, but she'd barely seen him before she was attacked.

Then she left.

Ted was the first to greet her once she made it to the kitchen. He had coffee and the paper in front of him. His attention was focused on an ad for a sale at the hobby store in the city.

"You should make those into flowers," she said, motioning to the newspaper. Cassandra had picked up on the fact that Ted Murphy was a man who enjoyed trying new things to do. "Megan Hamilton makes different flowers out of the paper. I've seen them. They're pretty cool. She said they're complicated enough to keep you focused but not troubling enough to make you swear." She winked. "Most times."

Ted eyed his paper again.

"I've never tried making anything with paper."

"Could be something there, Pops."

Jones came in through the doorway behind them. Carlos brought up the rear. There was a file under Jones's arm. He extended his smile to her.

Cassandra got all warm again.

"Morning," he said to her. "Do you want me to make you anything for breakfast? I'm a mean egg scrambler."

The man was definitely well-rested. Or, at least, not as dragged down as he had been. She was glad he'd gotten the rest.

"The doughnuts did the trick. But thank you."

"You can thank Bonnie for that. Her doughnut vice pays well for the rest of us." He turned to Carlos. "Want some coffee?"

"Are you kidding me? I'm now thinking about those mean scrambled eggs and doughnuts."

Both men laughed.

"The lady gets the good eggs, the kid gets dibs on the last doughnut and the man gets the coffee because I saw him woof down a sausage biscuit in his car."

Carlos pretended to take offense.

"Look at the 'towering sheriff' out here humbling me."

That got everyone laughing. Jones went to the coffeepot and, for a few minutes, Cassandra forgot about the rest of the world.

It didn't last long.

Ted went into the backyard to play with Bonnie while the rest of them hung around the dining-room table. The file beneath Jones's arm landed on the top.

"All right, we have our hands in a bunch of pies right now." Jones was addressing her, but Carlos was listening with rapt attention. "The department is looking after the Taurus that ran me off the road, also trying to figure out the Jimmy angle of it all. New Beginnings has eyes on it, same with the bunker and the McHales. Killian has Foster on him and, last I checked, the sketch artist should be coming into the department this morning to meet with Lottie to get a sketch on him since she's left the hospital already. Then there's the note."

Jones opened up the folder and spun a piece of paper around and out of it.

Cassandra recognized it as the paper that had been next to her phone in New Beginnings. The one signed by Annie.

"This is what we're going to focus on here." Jones tapped the signature twice.

"You want us to focus on Annie," she offered.

Jones nodded.

"The gardener who said he saw Annie on her last morning lied. I'm sure of it now, even without confirmation from the Deacon household and the schedule that Vera Lohan talked about. I'm not convinced, though, that this lie is relevant. He could have genuinely been mistaken and here we are chasing it as a lead for no reason. Though, it did lead us to the library and New Beginnings. Either way, it stands that Annie's parents saw her last, before the ransom demand."

"That's if no one else lied." Cassandra said it as an under-her-breath thought, but Jones agreed with it.

"Exactly," he said. "Before now no one even knew about Annie's friendship with Jasmine Lohan, definitely not their library scheme. I think we only got what we did by accident since Vera's memory has been coming and going. It might also have been why Vera left town."

"To keep the chances of her slipping up down," Carlos added.

"It's possible. Then again, people do move for reasons unrelated to Annie," Jones said, playing devil's advocate. "Regardless."

He tapped the paper again.

"Jasmine gave us the info on the library. Maybe she knows more."

Carlos nodded. "I can have her brought in."

"No," Jones said, the single word coming out sharp and fast. "I don't want to spook her. I'll find a way to get to her."

He paused.

"This whole thing has blown a weird hole into what we thought of Annie. Whoever wrote this might have known what was really going on or know enough to use Annie's name to make us jump when they say go and that's what we need to figure out. Who might do this, what was Killian's plan, who let the girls out of the bunker, and what might be their next steps."

Carlos nodded and put down his writing pad, pen already out. Jones settled at the head of the table, pulling his file closer to him.

Cassandra finally said a thought that had been floating around in her head since she'd woken in the bunker. It was quiet but impactful.

"Or it *is* Annie."

Jones and Carlos's heads snapped at attention.

"If she went to the library only to use the room for cover to go to New Beginnings, and if Killian was a patient there at the same time, then maybe they were seeing each other. And if they were seeing each other then, maybe they're seeing each other now."

Carlos's brow furrowed.

"We checked the timeline of his stay, the murders at the Rosewater Inn and Annie's kidnapping," he said. "Other than Lottie and her father, we can't find anyone else to even confirm Killian *was* a patient. It's possible Annie was sneaking in to see him or knew someone who let her in, just like Lottie. We have no evidence to back it up, though."

"If she was seeing Killian, then this goes back to who the hell is this guy?" Jones had his hands fisted on the table. "And, if he's tied to Annie somehow and Annie is working with him, or against him, or doing anything at all in the shadows, this town is going to burn at the knowledge."

Carlos nodded. Cassandra didn't understand.

"Wouldn't it be a good thing to know that Annie is alive after all of these years?"

"No."

The one syllable was hard, unmoving.

Jones took a second to explain.

"Annie's kidnapping might have opened our eyes to

all of the bad in this town, but it also created a lot of bad, too." His jaw clenched.

He was talking about the ambush at the park.

Helen's death.

"If Annie's kidnapping was a lie? If it was some kind of game or setup?"

"The Annie McHale this town has been praising for years will go from the angel of this town to its villain." Jones's frown was deep, severe. He snapped. "Just like that."

THE CONVERSATION COOLED as the three of them put their heads together for theories. An hour in and none were panning out. Carlos left for the department soon after and Cassandra went to the backyard to stretch her legs by walking around with Bonnie.

Jones watched them in deep conversation, trying to still piece together the mystery. It's why his father surprised him when he spoke at his side.

"I got up last night for some water and noticed you weren't on the couch or in Bonnie's room."

Jones sighed.

"I'm not talking about this right now, Dad."

His father shrugged.

"I didn't ask you to, now did I? I was just making an observation, is all. But, since I'm here, I'll make another one." He nodded out the window. "She's got the heart for this, you know?"

Jones lifted an eyebrow.

"This? You mean talking to Bonnie about the show

Bluey or her fascination about how turtles breathe through their butts?"

Jones was joking. His dad wasn't.

"All of this. Bonnie, you, sheriff, Kelby Creek. Being a mom. She has the heart for it and I wanted to make sure you realized it. Though, I think you already do."

Jones had woken up that morning and hadn't been able to wrap his head around the kiss the night before.

Why had he done it now?

Why hadn't he done it earlier?

But what had been a more pressing question was, why had she accepted him?

And was that what she'd done?

Or had she just been tired and gone along with it?

Jones sighed.

"It's that heart I'm worried about."

His father surprised him with a laugh.

"We've both had the privilege of sharing our lives with two wonderful women. To find someone else to love? That's an absolute gift, son. Don't waste it because you can't get out of your own head. I think your mother and Helen would tell you the same if they could."

Jones felt his father's hand on his back.

He often missed his mother, but he never once was ungrateful for his father's presence.

He let his dad give him a good, reassuring pat, until the moment ended by Jones's phone ringing.

"I'm going to make some snacks now so Bonbon doesn't become a sea monster. Try not to stress too much, if you can."

He went back to the kitchen while Jones took his call in the living room.

"Murphy here."

He didn't recognize the number but he did the voice.

"You're not going to believe this hot garbage, Sheriff."

It was Detective Howard.

Lily had never called his cell before.

"Hot garbage? Be more specific."

Lily went to talking fast.

"Jimmy just got out on bail with the fanciest lawyer I've ever seen. Some man from Birmingham with a suit Marco and my husband, Ant, agreed cost more than our cars combined. So, Juliet goes and asks Nan the million-dollar question—how in the devil's name could they afford this guy—and *Nan* tells her that it's none of her dang business and I've been digging deep and I can't figure out why this guy took the case and how he's being paid for it. I mean, this guy stabbed the sheriff. It's hot garbage that he's apparently out and has been since this morning. I mean, it's also Sunday, for gosh sakes."

Jones had tensed on the first part, and at the end he joined in on her confusion.

"Text me the name of the lawyer and the judge who signed off on this," he said. "Do we know where Jimmy is now?"

Lily seemed a might happier with the next news.

"Ant saw him first over near the restaurant and is sitting out there waiting. Don't worry, he's good at being sneaky, but I'd like to head out there myself since I'm not doing anything here that needs me tied to a desk."

Jones was nodding hard.

"Go on out and keep an eye on him for now. I still don't know what his deal is, but maybe you can catch him meeting with someone or doing something that gives us some insight."

"Will do, Sheriff."

They ended the call and Jones felt all the hotter for it.

Jimmy's attack and threat had been weighing on everyone. Now, given the last two weeks, Jones wasn't sure if he was a target, Cassandra was a target, some combination of the two, or if Jimmy had had one hell of a day when he'd brought a knife out at the department.

Either way, as Jones walked back into the kitchen he reaffirmed his stance that he wasn't leaving his family unattended.

He certainly wasn't leaving Cassandra alone.

Not while Killian was out there.

It was a stance that was immediately put to the test.

Bonnie came in, but Cassandra was still outside on her phone.

Her brow was creased. She was upset.

"It's Keith," Bonnie exclaimed before he could ask what was going on. "He called Miss West. He's crying!"

His dad appeared with a plate of chopped fruit. He gave Jones worried eyes.

"Then let's give her some space, Bonbon," he said. "This sounds like an adult problem to solve."

Bonnie agreed but looked out the window before she followed him.

"You don't leave your friends behind," she told Jones. "It's the pirate code."

"We're not leaving anyone behind," he assured her. Jones's gut was on high alert. He swooped down to give Bonnie a kiss on the head before going out to Cassandra.

She was ending her call.

"That was Keith." Worry was vibrating through her. "He said that Lila is crying in the kitchen. He asked if I'd come over and see them."

"Is *he* okay?"

She shrugged.

"I asked and he said he is, but his little voice was wobbling." She looked at the house behind him for a second. "Jones, I know you have a lot going on, but I'd really like to go see them. Poor Keith's been through a lot, never mind Lila."

Jones nodded.

"Let's go."

"I can't ask you to leave Bonnie and your father."

Jones pulled out his phone.

"I'm not leaving them alone."

He scrolled to Sterling's number.

"Still, I can't ask—"

Jones cut her off.

"You aren't asking me to do anything. I'm telling you that I already had a plan in place if I needed to leave the house."

He hit the call button but kept his eyes on her.

"Plus, we don't leave our friends behind."

Cassandra nodded.

"Pirate's code."

"Pirate's code," he repeated.

Chapter Nineteen

Lila and Joel lived in a one-road neighborhood five minutes from downtown. It was a quiet few houses, helped in part by the good amount of yard space between them, and Lila's was smack-dab in the middle. It was a nice two-story home with a cute Welcome sign and a stack of ceramic pumpkins on the porch.

The festive decorations didn't strike a festive mood.

It was cold outside and the clouds reflected it in their varying shades of gray.

That feeling had found its way into Cassandra's stomach.

She wrung her hands together as they parked at the curb.

"I'm sure they're fine. Nothing we can't help."

Jones's one hand enveloped both of hers.

He squeezed.

The worry abated. But only a little.

"And Bonnie and Ted have someone with them?" she asked. Again.

Jones didn't seem to mind the repeat. He helped her out of the car.

"Sterling, Marigold *and* Juliet."

"Won't that mess up the investigation?"

"Not at all. Juliet's a pro at phone duty. She can find out more using a cell than most people can sitting in front of a big screen. Dad's going to set her up in the house and Sterling and Marigold are going to stand guard outside. Don't worry about them."

She *was* worried about them, but at his confidence, Cassandra allowed herself to switch tracks.

Jones knocked on the door, but made sure to step aside when it opened to reveal Keith.

His little eyes instantly went to her, just as Cassandra instantly crouched to get to his level.

"Oh, Keith, what's wrong?"

The little boy's eyes were red and rimmed with tears. His cheeks had stains across them. Otherwise, he seemed in good physical health.

He didn't seem at all happy to see them, though.

He looked up at Jones.

"I didn't call you." Cassandra was taken aback at the tone in his voice. It was hard. She'd never heard it from the boy.

"This is Jones, remember him? He's my friend. I asked him to come to help. He knows Mrs. Lila, too. He can help."

Keith looked absolutely lost for a moment. Like he'd escaped into his own head and almost didn't come back out.

Cassandra shared a look with Jones.

He'd already picked up on what she was thinking.

"Hey there, Keith. I'm Bonnie's dad, too. She couldn't

come to check on you so she sent me. Why don't you let me go inside and talk to Mrs. Lila now, okay?"

He didn't wait for Keith to agree or not. Cassandra moved in tandem with him. She reached out to take Keith's hand. It was clammy with sweat but he held her fast. Cassandra stood and gently pulled him out and onto the porch.

Jones gave her a quick nod and disappeared into the house.

Cassandra shut the door softly behind him before focusing on the boy. She lowered herself again and squeezed his hand.

Keith took one look at the gesture and burst into tears.

"Oh, Keith, what's going on?"

The boy shook his head. Cassandra used her other hand to steady it.

"Keith, you can talk to me," she said softly.

But Keith wasn't having it.

He took his hand out of hers so quickly that Cassandra had to rock back on her heels so as not to fall over. She stood to keep the momentum from sending her down again.

Seeing her almost fall did something to the boy.

He slowed his breathing and seemed to be actively trying to stop crying.

It wasn't working but he did manage to talk through his tears.

"He—he made me do it," he stuttered out. "He said he'd hurt her if I didn't—didn't do it."

Cassandra's stomach, already cold, became a frozen wasteland in an instant.

"Who's he? Joel?"

Keith shook his head hard.

"I don't—I don't know him. He just told me to do it and I had to."

Cassandra heard the change in her own voice.

It pitched low, quiet.

"What did he make you do, Keith?"

Images of Lila crying filled her head.

Cassandra never imagined his answer.

"He—he told me to—to get you here."

The timing couldn't have been more perfect.

And maybe that was the point.

Footsteps thundered up behind Cassandra. Keith shrunk back and uttered one last thing through his tears.

"I'm—I'm sorry."

THE HOUSE WAS WARM, the lights were nice and it smelled like cinnamon.

It was a complete contrast to the awful scene he found in the downstairs bedroom.

"Lila!"

Keith's foster mom was tied to a recliner, facing the door. Her head was drooping down, but Jones could see the blood and bruises. Just as he could see the same around her wrists, where she was tied to the chair arms.

"Lila," Jones said again. He crouched down and gingerly lifted her chin. Her eyes remained closed. Jones felt for a pulse next.

It was there.

Barely.

"Hang in there, Lila," he told the unconscious woman.

He took his phone out again and immediately back-tracked through the house toward the front door. There was no way Keith had done that. Something else was going on.

Dispatch answered when he was next to the stairs.

Jones barked out for an ambulance and assistance, but didn't get to finish explaining what he'd found.

The front door burst open and Cassandra ran in.

She was dragging Keith and yelling.

"Jones!"

It was the only thing she could get out before Jones focused on her reason for running.

Jimmy was behind her, gun out.

Jones reacted on instinct.

He dropped his phone and ran at Jimmy, and in the space between put himself in front of Cassandra and Keith's backs.

Jimmy's eyes widened at the sight of Jones coming to meet him. Still, he looked as though he was about to pull the trigger.

There were cons to being well over six feet tall, but there were definite pros, too. In this case it meant a large wingspan and strides that got him to where he needed to be faster than the average man.

Jones made it to the gun before Jimmy could squeeze a bullet off. He managed to push the man's arm up just enough that the bullet went into the entryway ceiling and not Jones or the two he was protecting behind him.

Jimmy tried to correct his misfire but Jones wasn't having it.

He threw a left hook so hard it knocked the man off balance. He released his hold on the gun. It clattered against the hardwood.

Jimmy staggered back as Jones went for it.

This time he could see the knife coming.

Jimmy let out a war cry much like he had in the interrogation room at the department and struck out. Jones jumped back to avoid the hit, but ran into a wall.

Jimmy ran the knife deep into his shoulder.

Jones yelled out in pain and Jimmy had the audacity to gloat.

"Killing you will be as nice as killing her," he sneered, pushing the knife with all that he had.

Too bad for him he'd chosen very poor last words.

Jones wrapped his hand around Jimmy's holding the knife. Instead of trying to push off the man, Jones kept him there.

Once again, that wingspan was saving the day.

Jones used his other hand to grab Jimmy's head. His thumb pressed into the man's eyeball.

Jimmy yelled out in pain and tried to pull away, but Jones held him fast. He clawed at Jones's hand on his face.

"Nothing but small men hurt women," Jones growled.

He let go of Jimmy's hand and face, and the man staggered back, still yelling.

Jones knew his wingspan well, his stride, and his resolve to see that bad men like Jimmy never got a second chance.

But what he knew most of all, had spent his entire life learning?

It was how powerful he could be when he wanted.

Jones stood to his full height and brought up his fist.

"But big men like me have no problem returning the favor."

Jones wanted a knockout and that's exactly what he got.

His fist collided with Jimmy in a spectacular crack.

The other man crumpled to the ground in an instant.

Jones didn't waste time. He got the discarded gun and took it apart just as quickly.

"Cassandra?" he called out. "Are you okay?"

Movement from the room across from him caught his eye. Cassandra nodded; Keith's hands could be seen around her.

Her eyes widened. She clutched at her shoulder.

"Are you okay?" she asked, voice wobbling.

Jones turned and pulled the knife from him. He sucked in a breath.

"Yeah, I'm okay, just a little—"

Footsteps hit the porch.

Jones kept the knife in his hand and raised it, turning once again to block Cassandra and Keith from view.

This time, the man holding the gun held it with distance in mind.

Ray's face turned as pale as a ghost as he stopped outside of the opened front door.

He didn't even look down at Jimmy's prone body between him and Jones when he spoke.

"They got Lottie, Sheriff. Took her from my hands

like it was nothing." Ray's voice shook, but not enough to suggest he was about to break. He was steady, deliberate.

Jones didn't understand.

"Who took her? And how?"

Ray moved his head from side to side, but kept his aim true.

"I don't know. She got discharged from the hospital and we were at her house and one second she was there, the next she wasn't. Then I got a call and a man told me only one way to get her back." Ray continued to calmly hold the gun. But now, he moved it to the side and aimed it right at Cassandra and Keith. "I take her with me now and give you a chance to get her back later, or he takes your daughter and you'll never see her again."

Jones's heart dropped.

Ray didn't look pleased with his words.

He said as much.

"If it isn't me holding this gun, it'll be someone else, and there's nothing the two of us can do about it."

"You can put the gun down," Jones yelled out. He realized he'd never hung up his phone.

Where was it?

Was Dispatch hearing this?

Ray shook his head. He changed his gaze to Cassandra. He also changed his aim back to Jones.

"He can get you back later. If you don't come with me now, then he'll never leave this house." To put a deadly emphasis on his words, he cocked the gun.

"Wait! No, stop!"

Cassandra's footsteps were fast. Jones reached out

to her. Blood from his hand skimmed along her jacket in the process. It was a horrible contrast.

"No, Cassandra," Jones growled, but she was looking at Ray.

"How does he get me back?"

Ray opened his mouth, but someone else spoke over him. Someone from behind them.

A woman.

Jones wanted to turn his head to look at the new voice, but Ray still had his gun on him. If he decided to use it, Jones had to be ready to react.

"Ray Cooke, you put your gun down right now or it'll be you who doesn't leave this house," she said. "You and I both know that Lottie would rip you into two if you used a pregnant woman and a child as a bargaining chip for her."

"He'll kill her," Ray said, visibly breaking. "He said he would if I didn't do what he wanted."

The voice got closer.

It was strong and as steady as steel.

"It might be in his name, but Killian won't touch a hair on that woman's head. He's been in love with her since he first set eyes on her when they were kids. The only people he's planning on killing are you, me and these two lovebirds and their kids. If you help him now, then you're only hurting the same people who are going to help get Lottie back. So put that gun down so I don't have to shoot you in front of this kid. He's already going to have nightmares because of this idiot Jimmy."

Whether for effect or not, Cassandra put her hand on her stomach, cradling their unborn son.

Ray eyed the move.

Then he dropped his arm and let the gun go loose.

"Now, give that to Sheriff Murphy here. And, Keith? Could you take these to the sheriff to use on Ray there?"

Keith made a noise that must have been a yes. Soon after Jones felt his hand and something cold in his.

They were handcuffs.

"I'm sure you have some in your car, but I don't want you getting a chance to run off or fight me yet. So go ahead and make sure Ray doesn't make any other foolish decisions in the name of love. And, Ray, I'm going to need you to slide that gun off the porch before he gets to you, okay?"

Jones didn't like the orders, but he followed them. He wasn't the only one. The gun was already sliding away from Jones as he took Ray's arms and put them behind his back. He cuffed the man's wrists. When he turned back around the woman had positioned herself directly behind Cassandra, obscuring her face.

But not her voice.

"Now, Sheriff, I want you to bring Ray inside here and shut the door because I already have some bad news for you and we need to talk it out."

Jones stood still. He'd had enough. His shoulder ached, his head filled with angry resolve.

"I'm not moving until you tell me who you are. Plain and simple."

Cassandra nodded to him, agreeing with the directive.

The woman, who he expected to fight it, let out a

low sigh. She took a step to the side so Jones could finally see her face.

In that moment he felt a lot of things.

But, all he could say was a name.

"Annie McHale."

The woman smiled.

"In the flesh."

Chapter Twenty

Seeing a ghost would have been less jarring; seeing Annie McHale, alive, after six years, had the room so shocked that only the sheriff could break the silence.

And even then, Cassandra heard the great effort behind his words.

"This is Annie McHale," Jones said to the group that had formed in the room around them. Although she needed no introduction. They were all locals. They had known Annie for most of their lives. "Along with me and Cassandra, you now are the only people who know she's alive."

Jones didn't take his eyes off Annie. He hadn't since she'd shown herself. He wasn't the only one. Cassandra looked around Jones's father's living room and the people who had been contacted by Jones over the last fifteen minutes. All were law enforcement. Specifically from his department.

Lily Howard had an open face, but her brow was drawn—she was ready to take in whatever was said with great detail. Kenneth Gray was right there with her, standing with his arms crossed over his chest, jaw tight. Foster Lovett was in his street clothes with an impassive face, his wife, Millie, at his side, though she had originally come for Keith, who was with Bonnie in her room, and he was all worry. Kathryn Juliet was at their side, standing.

And angry.

It radiated off her so clearly that Jones had given her a quick word as everyone filed in.

Carlos, a man she'd only ever seen as even-tempered, looked stuck between being professional and joining Juliet.

Sterling Costner rounded out the group. His cowboy hat softened his severe expression, but only a little.

Then there was Jones Murphy, Sheriff.

Cassandra already knew what it meant to see Annie, alive.

He didn't know if the town's golden star was the bad guy or not.

And it was eating him up while he was having to force himself to listen and let that someone take control for a little bit.

Annie knew she held that power, too.

Cassandra could see it in her demeanor.

How had she gone from the girl who triggered The Flood to the young woman sitting in front of them like they were at a normal social event?

Annie, to her credit, addressed Jones with a more respectful tone than she'd given Ray.

Ray had been squirreled away to the department by Deputy Rossi, even though he still wanted to search for Lottie, while Lila and Jimmy had gone to the hospital with Deputy Marigold. As per Annie's request, and Jones's great hesitance, they were keeping the incident quiet.

For now.

All he'd managed was the barest of medical treatment for his shoulder from one of the EMTs who had shown up at Lila's. It was a quick bandaging job followed by a promise to Cassandra that he'd get it checked out more thoroughly as soon as possible.

"There's a few other people who actually know I'm alive," Annie began. "Of those, Killian Carmichael is our real problem."

"Who is he?" Jones's voice was even. He'd found calmness.

Annie didn't hesitate.

"He's my brother."

Everyone stayed quiet, but there were a lot of heads turning this way and that.

"I've never heard anything about the McHales having another child," Jones responded.

"I missed the news, too. Killian isn't just the skeleton in my family's closet. He's the graveyard." Annie didn't have her gun anymore, but she didn't need it to have their rapt attention.

"I found out about Killian by accident," she continued. "My parents were arguing. This, despite public opinion, was a common thing in our house, but when I realized it was them arguing about moving out of Kelby Creek, I listened. My mom didn't want to go but my father kept on, saying that we could all just leave it behind. I was young and dumb and self-absorbed, so

I thought they were talking about leaving silly things behind. Pageants, town fairs, ribbon cuttings, that kind of thing. But then, my mom said that they couldn't just leave 'him' behind."

Annie laughed. It wasn't in humor.

"It drove me crazy. That one little word. Like a song you can't get out of your head or an actor's name you just can't place. So I tried to figure it out. I asked them directly, at first, which only really sold me on digging deeper. My dad blew up. My mom got so nervous she knocked over a new glass of sweet tea. After that I noticed they also started keeping a better eye on me. I couldn't go two steps without needing a handful of excuses."

She shook her head.

"They kept acting so weird that I started looking into them. A hard thing to do to the most *beloved* couple in all of town." Her words were angry. She almost spit them before returning to her normal tenor. "But, being who I was and having money definitely helped. I found my way into not one secret but tons of them. My 'flood' happened months before yours, I just didn't realize how bad it was until I found him. Killian Carmichael, a teenager locked away in a mental health facility partially owned by his parents."

She snorted.

"Once you've pulled the curtain back on the lovely McHales, you realize that one of the problems of their *generosity* is that they somehow now own almost everything. Every gift, every good deed, was them trying to tip the scales of karma in their favor for when the world finally found out about their long-hidden son."

"Why keep him hidden?" Jones's voice was deep. It shook the room out of the trancelike state they'd fallen into.

Annie didn't seem to mind.

"He was the product of an affair by my mother," she answered. "Not the most original soap-opera-y thing to happen in this town, but it was enough to send my father into deep resentment. It only helped matters that as Killian got older he showed some sociopathic tendencies. As far as I could find, he lived at the house when I was little until he was moved to New Beginnings."

"The bunker."

Cassandra said it without question.

Annie nodded.

"If the McHales say they're building a storm shelter, who's going to question them? The town who loves them?" She snorted again. "But I didn't know any of this until after I'd already found Killian. He knew who I was instantly. Told me that our parents were the crazy ones and that I wasn't safe as long as I stayed with them. I believed him. After all, they'd been lying to me my whole life. I went to visit Killian every week and he spent those moments telling me about all the bad he'd learned about them. About how we were going to come up with a plan to help him escape or convict them so we could be free together."

For the first time, Annie looked wistful.

Sad.

Wishing for a different outcome to a story that was about to get bad.

"Then, one day, he said he'd been out. That escaping for him was possible. I didn't believe him until Lottie showed up. She didn't know I was there. I listened as he talked to her about the Rosewater Motel murders. I could hear her tone change, saw her face. Just like I saw Killian, and I knew. I knew that while my parents lied, they hadn't lied about everything."

"He killed them." Kenneth was the one who spoke this time.

Annie nodded.

"And then, I made another mistake." She looked at Jones directly. "I told my godfather."

"Sheriff Barkley." Jones had ground out the name.

The man who had betrayed the entire department, the entire town.

She nodded.

"He said he'd handle it and I went back the next morning to see if Killian was still there," she said. "He wasn't, but the sheriff was."

Annie paused and seemed to consider her next words.

"I know my being here, alive, might make a lot of you here angry," she said after a moment. "That if I'm walking around like nothing ever happened, then who did the kidnapping? If I wasn't really taken, then that means some of you lost a lot." Her eyes trailed back to Jones. They were shining. "But I'm here to tell you, he really did take me and I really did try to escape. I just couldn't until they grabbed Jackie."

No one spoke for a moment.

Cassandra knew that being the only one who wasn't a local gave her an emotional advantage. She spoke up and no one seemed against it.

"The FBI agent who went missing, you mean."

Annie nodded.

"She figured out the sheriff was behind it and then she was drugged. They put her in a chair next to me and she fought them off with everything she had. She told me to run and—and I did. I never saw her after that. But I tell you, I've spent all these years looking."

Cassandra stood, her hand on her belly. She wanted answers for the people around her. The one that could change everyone's minds about the woman.

"And what else were you doing all these years, Annie? Why not come forward and tell your story?"

Annie opened and closed her mouth, twice. She dropped her chin a little. For a moment, she truly looked like a girl, lost and alone.

"I didn't know who to trust after The Flood, especially with Killian out there. So I left for a while. I waited to see what the investigations would bring up… but then nothing happened. I realized that everyone here was working with half of the board, they couldn't see the whole picture because this town put one family on a pedestal so high up they never thought to do anything but praise them." Annie was crying now. Tears ran down her cheeks, but her voice was strong. "So when my parents left town—no doubt knowing exactly what happened to me and worried that it would come back on them—I came back to help the only way I thought I could. In the background, as a ghost."

"You've been in Kelby Creek, trying to help us, for six years?" Foster asked.

Annie nodded.

"Then what made you come out now?" Carlos asked next.

Annie's whole demeanor changed. It hardened. She wiped at her tears with her hand.

"Two sheriffs came to this house and I knew that they were going to ask Jones to be the next one." She adjusted her gaze to Jones. "And I knew you'd accept. Just like I knew you'd look into my kidnapping again. It seemed like a full-circle kind of sign and time to come forward. I guess Killian got wind of it and decided the same. I've been trying to figure out what he's planning while also being a step or two behind."

"You wrote the note at New Beginnings."

Annie shook her head.

"No. He did. But when he let me let you and Lottie out, I finally realized what he wants."

"He wants us to know you're alive." It wasn't a question. Jones's words were definite.

"I think he wants to come out of the shadows, condemn our family and use me as the catalyst. I think that's why he's using other people for his dirty work. Trying to keep his hands as clean as possible. I'd bet he already has someone framed up for it."

"And he can't come out of the shadows if we know what he looks like," Jones added.

"And me and Lottie are the only people who have seen him," Cassandra realized. "That's why he took her. Why he wants me."

Jones growled.

Annie spoke before he could follow that with words.

"This is where the bad news I was talking about comes in."

"You mean none of this has been bad news?" Carlos asked.

Annie ignored the comment.

She was back to Jones.

"Killian is smart. He's going to see this through. The only way we can stop him and make every McHale pay for what they've done—what they've covered up—through the years... Ray already told you where he was supposed to take Cassandra. Why not see it through?"

Jones shook his head in one aggressive no.

He went taut with tension.

"No way am I taking her there."

Cassandra knew his immediate dismissal was more than warranted. Ray had admitted he was supposed to exchange Cassandra for Lottie at the park.

The same one where the ransom exchange and ambush happened all those years ago.

The same place where his wife had been killed.

It was a hard ask and maybe that was why Killian had chosen it.

The park was a sore spot for most of the town.

"If we just go in guns blazing, he might run. He might not even be there."

"He might also shoot her on sight."

Annie stood up. She pointed to Cassandra.

"He needs her first. He needs her to draw me out, just like he did when he left that note at New Beginnings. He knew I wasn't going to stay hidden when I saw he'd taken her and Lottie. He'll only get her after I'm out in the open and we're all going to make sure that doesn't happen."

"Then go reveal yourself to him," Jones growled. "If he wants to draw you out, just step up and let him see you! No need to put anyone else at risk." His frustration was palpable.

Annie shook her head.

"That's not how he works. He's not some rational man. It's his way or no way. We either play his game or it's game over for Lottie. I wish it wasn't the case but, it is. We need Cassandra if we want Lottie. If we want him."

Jones was violent with the no this time. His voice was concrete.

Yet that's not what made his words so startling.

"I am *not* losing another woman I love to that place, especially not when she's carrying our son."

The room, minus Annie, quieted.

Those from the sheriff's department weren't coy with their looks of surprise.

Cassandra wasn't coy with hers, either.

Annie, though, didn't care.

She wanted justice.

She wanted six years of her life alone to matter.

She wanted the town that broke because of her family to find some kind of peace.

And, by God, if Cassandra didn't want that for her.

For all of them.

For the man she'd fallen for the second he'd agreed to play the question game in that hotel.

For their future, their son, Bonnie, Ted, Keith...

Cassandra took a step forward. She placed her hand on Jones's arm.

Her words were as strong and definite as his.

"I'm going." Jones turned, mouth already opening, but she shook her head. "But only if you can answer this question honestly."

Cassandra nodded to the room behind them.

The men and women with badges who'd spent the last six years trying to redeem the department once riddled with corruption and betrayal.

"Do you trust *them*?"

Jones didn't like the question.

But, perhaps, he disliked the answer more.

"Yes."

Cassandra turned to Annie.

"Then let's do this."

Chapter Twenty-One

The park was beautiful. Always had been.

Good for walking, great for playing, the best for picnics.

That's why Helen had been waiting for him that day, on the grass, straightening out a picnic blanket next to the lunch she'd made for them. She didn't know about the ransom exchange and he hadn't known she was there.

Until it was too late.

Now, he had no excuse.

He knew what was happening and yet there Cassandra was, walking over the grass with Ray Cooke at her side.

"You can't control everything that happens," she had told him before they left. "No one person can. I want to do this. I want this all to end so we can be safe. So our kids can be safe. If me showing up does that, you need to let me."

"She'll be okay." Carlos was down to a whisper. That was the rule. If this plan was going to work, they needed to be like Annie.

They needed to be ghosts.

Jones kept watching Cassandra.

She was walking toward him.

Because everyone in the sheriff's department was currently hiding in the woods, the surrounding businesses and the park itself. Killian didn't realize it, but there was about to be a second ambush at the park, this time with the good guys in the lead.

At least, Jones hoped.

He believed Annie and her story. He just did. Right down in his gut.

To his surprise, though, it was a mutual feeling among his friends.

They'd gone to working on the plan faster than he'd ever seen them work.

Ray was released and told to play his part, saying that he and Cassandra had to hide from deputies until the coast was clear to come to the park, as if he'd lured Cassandra. They used an all-points bulletin for her along with one for him. Meanwhile, deputies were scouring the town everywhere but the park to look for them.

On the outside, it looked like Ray's plan had worked.

Jones just hoped it stayed that way until Annie could trap him.

Carlos tapped his elbow.

Cassandra and Ray were almost to the set of benches closest to the tree line.

Jones took out his gun and waited.

Carlos started looking around them while Jones watched Cassandra and Ray sit down on one of the benches.

Five minutes went by.

Then a few more.

Carlos tapped his elbow again, but this time with force.

Someone was walking through the woods next to them.

It was Lottie.

And a man Jones was guessing was Killian Carmichael.

He looked just like Annie but a bit taller and with long dark hair.

Snake in the grass was what came to Jones's mind at the sight of him. That and several other derogatory terms.

Killian was too confident. He was smirking as he pushed poor Lottie along.

He kept that smirk tight as Annie walked up, cutting him off from Cassandra and Ray.

"Well, well, I was wondering when the golden child would show." Killian's voice carried. "For a second I thought you were going to let me take the poor pregnant teacher without any fuss. Not very like you."

Annie's anger was real.

Her calm was, too.

She was ready for this.

So were they.

A text came in and lit up Carlos's phone.

Carlos repeated the message so low Jones barely heard it.

"Sterling found a silver Taurus across the street. A man is inside. They're surrounding it, but won't move until we say."

Jones nodded.

Good.

Annie had said there were two men working directly with Killian as far as she could tell. Jimmy and the man with the Taurus.

If they had them handled, then all that was left was Annie and Killian.

The siblings had finally stopped across from one another, but left enough space to show that they weren't about to trust that the other didn't have a weapon ready. Jones was surprised that Killian, for all of his planning, didn't have a gun out.

Then again, he thought he had the upper hand with Ray holding Cassandra.

"What do you want from me?" Annie asked. "What could I possibly give you that you don't already have? Mom and Dad already give you money to keep you away from them. You haven't been caught for the murders you've committed, the crimes you've helped orchestrate and fund. I mean, no one even knows who *you* are, Killian. You could leave now, let Lottie and Cassandra go, and never look back at Kelby Creek ever again. What could you possibly want?"

Killian wasted no time.

His answer was boiling.

"I want them to know *me*."

Jones almost stood as Killian pulled a gun.

Annie didn't flinch as her brother pointed it at her.

"I want them to see what I see, what I've seen," he continued. "I want this whole town to realize they've been worshiping the wrong McHales. That it's time they get to know me. The son who's spent his entire life trying to build a legacy that will crush Mom and Dad's. A legacy that shows I triumphed in the face of absolute adversity."

From his hiding spot, Jones could see the man's smirk rise again.

Killian's gun was on Annie.

"One that truly begins when I finally show the world just how wrong they've been about little Annie McHale. The girl who could have shown herself for years but instead let everyone suffer." He laughed. "But I suppose you already guessed how this little meeting was going to go. Which means you must already know how they'll treat you."

His smirk dropped.

"So are you here to join me, Annie, and beg for forgiveness? Or are you here to try and save the day?"

Jones stood to his full height. He nodded to Carlos.

Killian aimed his gun.

Annie took a second.

Then she smiled.

"I think the sheriff can save the day just fine."

A lot of things happened all at once.

Carlos told Sterling to get the man in the Taurus.

Cassandra, who was connected to Jones by Bluetooth earbuds and an open phone line, yelled to Ray to run.

Lottie, of her own instincts, ducked down.

And Jones, the Dawn County Sheriff, took one precise shot.

The sound ricocheted through the forest around them.

Killian Carmichael dropped to the ground, screaming.

Annie picked up his gun and Carlos rushed over with his.

Jones followed.

"Are you okay?" Cassandra's voice was in his ear, and it was the most beautiful sound he'd ever heard.

Before Jones could answer, the woods had men and women running inside to meet them, all guns pointed toward Killian.

"Are you okay?" Jones asked her instead.

"I'm okay."

Jones smiled at the men and women around him, then to Annie.

His trust had paid off.

He let out a sigh of relief.

"Then I'm okay, too."

A YEAR WENT BY.

Then three more.

Joshua was born, Keith was adopted and Bonnie finally got her a sister when Adriene came into the world one late night in November. Their family grew when his father married Megan Hamilton and, finally, it was time for Jones to fulfill an old dream and build a house big enough for all of the family and friends they had collected over the last four years.

It was that house that they were standing in now, party food out, music playing softly, that had them all laughing together.

Foster came in with Millie and their three kids, Carlos and Dr. Amanda Alvarez helped carry the baby. Amanda was pregnant with twins and Carlos had the sonogram framed on his desk next to their wedding picture. Marco Rossi, now captain at the department, came in with his wife, Bella, and their kids ran straight to Keith and Bonnie's rooms the second their feet were in the door. With Millie's help they'd adopted a brood of their own, two of their kids the same age as Bonnie and Keith.

Marigold and her boyfriend puttered in next, all tangled up in laughter with Sterling and his wife, Mel. Their daughters went to Bonnie's room faster than the earlier kids had. Kenneth and Willa's son at least said hi before he jetted off. Willa rubbed her pregnant belly and laughed at them.

"The only reason he stops and says hello is because of Lily and Ant's kids," she said. "Honest to goodness, they try to make everyone they meet smile."

Sure enough, when Lily and Anthony showed, their six kids sounded almost rehearsed as they yelled off hellos and how-do-you-dos.

Ant let out a loud boom of a laugh as Marigold explained why the rest of them were laughing.

Ray and Lottie came out of the kitchen, wondering what the fuss was all about. June and her wife yelled loudly over it all to say they were crazy for the sheer amount of children in the house, but Jones heard the smiles in it. Lila had once joined in with the mock jeering at so many kids but now she and her new husband, Charlie, were working on their second.

His dad, someone who thrived in a kid-filled house apparently, showed up with Megan and the party went on for a while as the best kind of chaos and noise.

Then the doorbell rang and most of the adults quieted when Jones answered the door.

"Sorry, I'm late."

Annie McHale sported a smile. It was one that Jones had come to recognize as sincere.

"Before I come inside, I was wondering if I could talk to you first?"

Jones, who'd had Adriene hanging on his leg, nodded to Cassandra. She swooped in with Joshua already on her and told Annie hello.

Annie returned the greeting and then waited for Jones to lead them to the corner of the wraparound porch.

In the last four years, she'd been through a lot.

Not as much as the six years before that, of course.

But enough.

After the recording of Killian admitting to what he'd done had come out, Annie had, too. What followed was an investigation into her, Killian and the rest of the McHale family that garnered no nickname, as The Flood had done.

Annie had been telling the truth.

So had Killian.

It took until his trial but he finally found a place he couldn't escape. He cooperated to reduce his sentence and, in the process, implicated his mother and father in several cover-ups and financial schemes that benefited them and them alone.

They'd also admitted, when their time came, that they had thought Killian had killed Annie and had been paying him for years to keep him away from them.

Jasmine Lohan had been brought in too for her involvement with Killian but had been given a deal for any information she'd had on him. He'd used her to try and get Annie through Cassandra but he'd also threatened her children in the process. No one, not even Jones and Cassandra, had ever blamed her for her part in the ruse.

She'd also implicated the man in the Taurus, Brandon Ross. He'd gone to school with her as a teenager and had struck up a friendship with Killian through the years. He hadn't cooperated and neither had Jimmy when it was his time to talk. It was only when Nan came forward that she admitted her brother had spent the last few years after The Flood growing more and more angry. He'd often said that he'd played by the rules that had been forced on him by the law for decades and The Flood had shown his innocence had been pointless. So, he'd tried to move on but every few months it seemed like the town was dragged back to the investigation into Annie McHale. Nan had admitted they'd both hated when that had happened. They'd agreed that it had sometimes felt like the sheriff's department was dragging the whole town back into the bad, making them suffer old wounds on repeat.

"I think all Jimmy had wanted to do was make y'all stop forcing us to relive it all," Nan had said. "He was trying to save the town."

Her testimony hadn't helped her brother. He'd tried to kill people, including a pregnant woman. There was no amount of good intention in that.

The trials had gone on for two years regardless. They

were made all the more complicated when the body of Agent Ortega had been found buried on the McHale property.

The investigation into Annie herself had ended that morning.

"I'm going to leave," she said now to Jones. "I've decided it's time to find my place in this world and it's not in Kelby Creek. Not anymore. I just wanted to be the first to tell you since you've done so much for me. You and Cassie. Thank you."

Jones had been expecting this. He didn't blame her for trying for a new start. Still, he was sad to see her go. He said as much.

"It'll be a lot less interesting without you around. I know we're all going to miss you."

Annie was still having trouble when it came to being vulnerable, but he saw her cheeks redden at the affection. Jones wanted to make sure she knew how much she really meant to the group.

He nodded back to the house.

"You hear all that in there?" he asked. "The yelling and general wildness of kids and their grown-ups?"

Annie laughed and nodded.

"That is, in a way, because of you. Because of what you did through the years. You helped all of us, at some point. Now, we're loud and outnumbered and, well, this town doesn't deserve you anymore, Annie, and I think there's some beauty in that."

Jones put a hand on her shoulder.

"I can't wait to see where you go next."

Annie was all blush.

She looked back at the house.

Cassandra had come outside.

"Sorry, I didn't want to interrupt, Jones, but Marco said he needs your help. Keith and Jordan might have gotten their heads stuck in the banister again."

Annie laughed.

"That I have to see." Annie walked back to the house, but Jones caught Cassandra's hand.

She was close enough to kiss, so he did.

It was perfect.

"So you want me to go rescue some kids from our banister again, huh? I guess I have to. We do have a code, after all."

Cassandra nodded.

She kissed him one more time.

"Pirate's code," she said.

He laughed.

"Pirate's code."

* * * * *

If you missed the previous books in the Saving Kelby Creek Series by Tyler Anne Snell, you'll find them wherever Harlequin Intrigue books are sold!

Uncovering Small Town Secrets
Searching for Evidence
Surviving the Truth
Accidental Amnesia
Cold Case Captive

 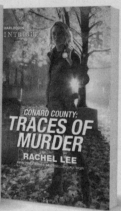

His hands cupped her face. She blinked up at him.

"They buried me," she said, fighting the emotion
trying to take over at the thought of never seeing him
again.

Anger flashed in his blue eyes, and his jaw muscles
clenched. "They better never touch you again. We can
make an excuse to get you out of here. Say one of your
family members is sick and you had to go."

"They'll see it as weakness," she reminded him. "It'll
hurt the case."

He thumbed a loose tendril of hair off her face.

"I don't care, Ree," he said with an overwhelming
intensity that became its own physical presence. "I can't
lose you."

Those words hit her with the force of a tsunami.

Neither of them could predict what would happen next. Neither could guarantee this case wouldn't go south. Neither could guarantee they would both walk away in one piece.

"Let's take ourselves off the case together," she said, knowing full well he wouldn't take her up on the offer but suggesting it anyway.

Quint didn't respond. When she pulled back and looked into his eyes, she understood why. A storm brewed behind those sapphire-blues, crystalizing them, sending fiery streaks to contrast against the whites. Those babies were the equivalent of a raging wildfire that would be impossible to put out or contain. People said eyes were the window to the soul. In Quint's case, they seemed the window to his heart.

He pressed his forehead against hers and took in an audible breath. When he exhaled, it was like he was releasing all his pent-up frustration and fear. In that moment, she understood the gravity of what he'd been going through while she'd been gone. Kidnapped. For all he knew, left for dead.

So she didn't speak, either. Instead, she leaned into their connection, a connection that tethered them as an electrical current ran through her to him and back. For a split second, it was impossible to determine where he ended and she began.

Don't miss
Mission Honeymoon *by Barb Han,*
available August 2022 wherever
Harlequin Intrigue books and ebooks are sold.

Get 4 FREE REWARDS!

We'll send you 2 FREE Books plus 2 FREE Mystery Gifts.

FREE
Value Over
$20

Both the **Harlequin Intrigue®** and **Harlequin® Romantic Suspense** series feature compelling novels filled with heart-racing action-packed romance that will keep you on the edge of your seat.

Love Harlequin romance?

DISCOVER.

Be the first to find out about promotions, news and exclusive content!

 Facebook.com/HarlequinBooks

 Twitter.com/HarlequinBooks

 Instagram.com/HarlequinBooks

 Pinterest.com/HarlequinBooks

You Tube YouTube.com/HarlequinBooks

ReaderService.com

EXPLORE.

Sign up for the Harlequin e-newsletter and download a free book from any series at **TryHarlequin.com**

CONNECT.

Join our Harlequin community to share your thoughts and connect with other romance readers!
Facebook.com/groups/HarlequinConnection